VADIM: CONTROL

A CLUB XXX NOVEL: BOOK FOUR

LANA SKY

Control

Control By Lana Sky

Copyright © 2020 by Lana Sky
All rights reserved.

No part of this publication may be reproduced, distributed, or transmitted in any form or by any means, including photocopying, recording, or other electronic or mechanical methods, without the prior written permission of the author.

This is a work of fiction. Names, characters, businesses, places, events and incidents are either the products of the author's imagination or used in a fictitious manner. Any resemblance to actual persons, living or dead, or actual events is purely coincidental.

Cover Design and Interior Formatting by Charity Chimni
Proofreading by Charity Chimni

ACKNOWLEDGMENTS

Thanks so much to everyone who supported this draft along the way, including the many beta readers who provided encouragement along the way! Please keep in mind that this story includes dark, graphic, and explicit content matter that is not suitable for readers under the age of 18—or for readers who are uncomfortable with the following subject matter: explicit sex, mentions of sexual abuse, mentions of child abuse, graphic depictions of violence, and mentions of self-harm.

CHAPTER ONE

When delving into the world of sexual promiscuity, it's totally okay to have *one* glass of wine beforehand, just to calm your nerves. Two is fine too. Okay, three—but there's a benefit to every sip of alcohol far beyond the use as a mental crutch.

Or so I tell myself.

For one, I'll be nice and loose for whatever millionaire I manage to snag on my first night on the prowl. Depending on how well it goes, I'll be closer to scratching the big-ticket item off my bucket list—joining a secretive, exclusive sex club. Through that act alone, I'll be giving my ex-husband the ultimate kiss-off, while indulging in years of repressed sexuality to boot.

Win, win.

Telling myself that makes it easier to down my fourth glass as I scan the offerings milling about the exclusive "Gray Bar" of Hotel Six—the most exclusive venue within ten miles of the area's major airport. It's a forty-floor haven for millionaire businessmen with too much money to spend and not enough time to look for a relationship lasting beyond a few hours. In theory, it should be a sexual revolution Mecca.

In reality, it's slim pickings tonight, go figure. The one night of the week I finally managed to gather up the nerve to assemble an outfit that—in the right lighting—makes me look like I almost belong here. Enough that I was able to slip past the stern-faced bouncer before he could do a double take.

Though, maybe I should have tried my skills on him first? The old guy could have been a nice warm-up for my rather lacking talent of seduction. Frowning, I do the math on my fingers. Six months since my divorce from Jim was final. Three years since we last had sex. Minus the odd dildo every now and again, I haven't been laid in…

Too damn long. Sighing, I let my fingers fall to the table before me and tap the polished wood with my hot pink nails. A normal person would try online dating, or maybe troll the grocery store for some horny single dad with a fetish for one-night stands to ease her way back into the dating pool. A normal person.

I, however, decided to skip the queue and jump into the big, wide world with a bang. Literally. Why feign interest in a long-term relationship or play the roulette game with STDs when you can aim right for the jackpot—exclusive millionaire sex clubs like the kind my uncle Conroy used to gossip about after one too many brandies.

The millionaire part is beside the point. Three big ones, actually —safety—both physically and health-wise—privacy and most importantly…kink. Weird, crazy kink. Enough to drown out say, seven or so years of a lifeless marriage and boring, missionary sex so lame that a nun wouldn't consider participating as breaking her vows.

Yes, Tiffy, I tell myself. *You're on a roll. A horrible, fruitless roll.*

An hour in, and I have yet to be approached by one of the three men occupying the lounge in addition to me. It must be the slow hour for rich bachelors.

One potential prospect sits at the bar, his back to me. A curtain of dark hair obscures most of his face, but he's scrawny. Too scrawny. *Next.*

Sighing, I shift my attention to another potential victim. Aged approximately seventy years, with a beautiful head of balding gray hair, he's only a moderately more appealing candidate. I bet rich old men have plenty of experience to draw from, though. Viagra can be a heck of a drug—and hell, to make their trysts last, those over sixty probably extend the foreplay too.

Bonus points.

Not that I would know how to recognize extended foreplay if it slapped me in the face. Jim thought oral sex was sinful—unless on the rare occasion he had two beers, it wasn't Sunday, and I was the one willing to open my mouth.

Stop it. I shake my head to clear away the negative thoughts—no more dwelling on the past. I'm the new and improved Tiffany Connors. No longer bitter about years of youth wasted. No longer hating on my prudish ex-husband. No longer sexually repressed.

So very sexually repressed.

I crane my neck to the corner of the room where the third and last potential victim sits thrumming through a magazine. The fact that it's Vogue, paired with his impeccably tailored suit, sends my gaydar pinging hard. *Strike three.*

After yet another sip of wine for courage, I cycle back to bachelor number one, the guy at the bar. He's not my type, but what's the harm in trying? Glass in hand, I leave my booth and approach him, praying to God I don't trip in these heels. It's the first time I've worn anything but neat, respectable flats in nearly a decade —yet another example of jumping headfirst into my new carefree life.

Forcing my lips into a friendly grin, I sidle up to my target. "Hello," I purr huskily—or at least I try to. "I'm Tiff."

He inclines his head toward me, and my eyelids flutter in shock. I'm so caught off guard; I nearly let my sexy rouse slip in favor of gaping at him.

He's pretty. Freakishly so. An angelic nose anchors his delicately crafted features—like a masculine but beautiful doll. Pale skin conforms to his high cheekbones and strong jaw. Jesus almighty, I've never seen a sexier jaw. Eyes so dark, I feel the need to strike a match take me in with little reaction, and my brain runs wild trying to decipher them. Is he bored? Surprised that I've approached him?

A half-empty glass of whiskey sits in front of him and nothing else—a testament to the brooding businessman stereotype.

Score.

"Gorgoshev," he says in a voice so rich my tongue dampens, my throat contracting. He has an accent I can't place. Russian, given the name? No. Something more musical. French? I'm too distracted to put much effort into narrowing it down as he extends his hand toward me.

And it's as beautiful and slim as the rest of him. My nails look garish against his porcelain skin, and I'm ten times more self-conscious. Way to make a first impression. If he already doesn't think I'm a dumb bimbo, I'm halfway there.

"Do…do you come here often?" I ask, flicking my hair over my shoulder. I must flick too hard because one of my hoop earrings smacks off my chin, and I nearly slip from my stool.

A cool hand catches my wrist before I can lose my balance completely, anchoring me in place.

"T-Thank you," I stammer, smoothing my fingers over my skirt. He moved so fast. Already he's back to nursing his whiskey as if he never budged at all. "I've probably had way too much wine."

I groan internally. The fact that I acknowledge drinking at all is a sign I've definitely had too much wine. Surprisingly, Mr. Pretty doesn't seem to mind my sloppiness.

My heart races the more I watch him, and I dare to hope this could be working. He's handsome enough, and yes, he may be freakishly thin, but I can work with it. Jim—no, not thinking about him. *My ex,* has the body of a college linebacker five years beyond his prime, so I'm not picky.

Smiling wider, I try to engage the non-cheating, non-asshole person before me in conversation. *Say something smart, Tiff.* "Is Gorgoshev your first or last name?" I wonder.

Kill me.

"Last," he says, either oblivious to the stupidity of the question or he must get it a lot. "I'm not inclined to give out my first name to strangers." A playful smirk shapes his mouth, softening the rejection hidden within his words. *Touché.*

"I'm Tiffany Connors," I blurt. It could be the wine talking, but something about him makes me curious enough to extend the conversation, all embarrassment aside. "Age twenty-eight. I like long walks on the beach. I can assure you that I'm not a serial killer—"

"And I'm sure you carry quite the reputation in finance to commandeer a private booth in such an establishment," he says over me.

I clam up as my cheeks catch fire. Smart man—*too* smart, it seems. "I…I…"

"Relax." He cocks his head back and takes a small sip from his drink. "You're the first woman under fifty to come in here alone —" He meets my gaze directly, and my heart lurches. "Pardon me for being curious."

"Oh, yeah…" I flick my tongue along my lower lip, weighing the benefits of further engagement. He seems nice, but his lack of ogling my tits or trying to feel me up leaves me puzzled. Navigating the dating world beyond high school is a brand-new experience for me. Are we in good territory? Bad? Should I cut my losses and move on to an easier mark like the bald guy across the room?

Decisions. Decisions.

Jutting my chin, I decide on the spot to cut the bullshit and go for the balls. "Maybe I'm not a financier," I confess, eyeing him through my lashes. "Maybe I'm interested in something a lot more fun than comparing business ventures. What do you say? I'll show you mine if you show me yours."

A part of me cringes inside—the good, God-fearing part of me that wishes I was wearing a nice sweater instead of a dress that exploits my cleavage to hell and back. After two years, it's still hard to shake the old girl.

But as Mr. Gorgoshev's eyes flicker from my face down to my collar, I suddenly can't hear anything but the hard swallow contorting my throat. Good girl Tiffy can put a sock in it.

"Vadim," he says. "First name."

"Vadim," I parrot, playing with the syllables. I probably sound more tipsy than sexy, but a thrill runs through me anyway. I swear his eyes narrow slightly. So I say it again.

"Are you alright?" he wonders, a black eyebrow raised.

"Huh?"

"Your voice. It sounds strange." Frowning, he takes another sip of his whiskey while I pray I might sink through the floor and die. Just when the mortification becomes unbearable, he flashes one of those disarming grins. "If I didn't know better... I'd think you were coming on to me, Ms. Connors."

A teensy bit of my panic gives way to an excited flutter in my belly. "And if I am?"

He seems to mull it over, his dark eyes gleaming. "Then I would have to say..." With undeniable interest, his gaze flits over me a second time, and my heart lurches. "How much?"

CHAPTER TWO

"M-Much?" I eye my glass of wine and feel my nose wrinkle. "To be honest, I haven't really been paying attention to the number of glasses I've—" My brain realizes what he's implying before my mouth does. The second I do, my teeth slam together as a horrible wave of mortification washes over me, so intense, so paralyzing that it brings with it a sensation of déjà vu.

Like the day I strolled past my beautiful white picket fence, in my old beautiful life, and walked up the porch of my beautiful house. And then I found my once beautiful husband sitting at the kitchen table beside his beautiful whore. The joke had been on me. After seven years of changing myself to please him, he'd decided to spring for a younger, newer model.

And together, they had presented their case for a divorce.

I told myself I'd never feel like that again. Not ever. Not even at the mercy of the mysterious figure I once considered fucking.

"I've offended you," he says, the second I lurch from my stool. "Explain."

Something in his tone forms a wall against the indignation prickling through my skin. It's like the world just shifted, and even though I'm the one insulted, he's managed to turn the tables.

"What makes you think I'm—" I glance at the bartender nearby and lower my voice, horrified. "A prostitute?"

His brows furrow, and once again, I feel like I'm the asshole. "You're beautiful," he points out in a tone that makes my brain sputter and anger go poof. "I'm not your type. I can tell by your body language—" He nods toward my legs, which were neatly crossed with my hands folded over them. "You'd be positioned toward me if I were. Therefore, a beautiful woman, in a lounge meant only for business professionals, confronting me directly even though she's not sexually attracted to me..." He smirks, letting the obvious hang in the air.

As Uncle Conroy would say, *"That's check and mate, Tiffy. Know when to quit."*

"Check please," I call to the bartender, fighting to keep my voice calm. "I'm sorry, I should go—"

"So soon?" I stiffen as, once again, his tone catches me off guard. Not insulted, I think. Just curious. "Whatever your price, I would have paid it," he adds offhandedly. "I have time to kill before my next flight."

I falter as two realizations clash in my brain. One, he really does think I'm a prostitute. Two, he's boldly stated his interest in sex. With me. Now. Sex, complete with a graceful escape built-in by way of him being guaranteed to leave afterward.

My irritation dissipates instantly. I feel like a kid who had Christmas literally fall into her lap.

"You could name your price," Vadim continues, sparing me another glance. He lingers this time, allowing a hint of appreciation to seep into his gaze where it lacked before. He's not my type—he was right about that. But there is something about him that makes me do a double take, paying particular notice to his mouth. It's just so damn pretty. His lips look soft too.

And my brain jumps straight into X-rated territory because restraint is a foreign concept to this new and improved Tiffy. He's probably amazing at oral. Not that I'd know what oral— amazing or otherwise—from anyone feels like. But that's the point of going on a sexual adventure, isn't it? The thrill of discovery.

"I should have known better, I suppose." Vadim sighs wistfully, his mouth quirked in another teasing smile. "A beautiful woman, approaching me in a lounge primarily inhabited by men older than this brand of scotch, at a particular time when I was considering finding myself a companion…" He stands and fishes a handful of crisp bills from the breast pocket of his suit, placing them onto the counter. "Of course, it was too good to be true."

He steps past me, emitting a scent of booze and cologne that hits my nostrils like a punch. It's so deliciously male. So…sexy.

Without thinking, I'm already following after him. "If I was a…" I can't even say it. "What would you think my 'price' would be?"

"Honestly?" He looks me over, his frown thoughtful. "A grand for the four hours," he says—but from his tone, I can tell that it's not a boast. It's an honest gosh darn guess.

"R-Really?"

"You're confident which betrays a familiarity with high-class clients," he deduces, stroking his chin as if interpreting me is a task requiring his full concentration. "I'm sure your agency keeps a list of your references, and judging from your outfit, you have the financial stability to be discerning."

My outfit. It's one of the few things I splurged on with my first few alimony payments. A hot pink faux fur jacket with a genuine *Sergio Demassi* red silk cocktail dress that cost so much money I couldn't even look at my bank account after. My shoes are vintage Chanel in a rare royal purple I managed to score from one of my mother's socialite contacts. As far as jewelry, well, the diamond necklace was a present from Uncle Conroy from about ten years back, but it still cuts a striking figure with the right outfit. One could say I'd gone overboard. On the trip here from my less exclusive, more modest hotel across town, I'd caught plenty of women glancing at me with barely concealed smirks.

I hadn't even blushed. Who cares? I'm free, and freedom comes with the ability to wear whatever the hell you want. And apparently, some rich, beautiful man thinks that I'm worth a grand for just four hours. The joke's on them.

"Wait!" I don't even realize he's halfway across the bar until I finally regain my senses enough to choke out a strangled, "Thank you."

He cocks his head, his steps slowing. "Please tell me you've reconsidered?"

Biting my lip, I think through my options. Explore this avenue a little more or go crawling back to my hotel room? Or, take my chances with baldy across the way. There is no competition.

"Come sit." I sink back onto my stool and crook a finger, beckoning him with a confidence that sends my inner Bible-self reeling. "You didn't even finish your drink."

I snatch up his glass before the bartender can clear it. Held beneath my nose, the smell packs a punch. It's well beyond the cheap stuff a teenage Tiffy might have smuggled from Mommy and Daddy's drink caddy. It's the good stuff. Very good. *Uncle Conroy-trying-to-impress-wife-number-six-with-his-wealth* good.

"You could finish it for me," Vadim suggests, appearing by my side. Dutifully, he regains his stool, copying my position with his back to the bar. "I should keep my head clear. I have a meeting in not too long."

Curious despite myself, I take a sip and promptly sputter. It tastes like nail varnish. Damn expensive, quality nail varnish.

"So, you're just passing through? Where are you headed?" I ask, my ears still ringing from the booze. Way, way more dangerous than a glass of wine. *Slow down, Tiffy,* my inner voice warns. But that voice isn't face-to-face with a man so pretty it hurts. I find him sexier the more I appraise him. After another tiny sip of whiskey, I'm wondering why I ever considered him unattractive in the first place.

There's something about his eyes that I find the most enticing. They're...shadowed. Like he has an invisible wall up, and I'm only seeing a sliver of what lurks underneath—what he wants me to see. And right now, he wants me to see a sheepish, devastating smile.

"Have you ever been?" he wonders.

"Huh?" Another sip of whiskey and my brain is practically buzzing. He could have drugged it, or so says the rapidly diminishing voice of good Bible-Tiffy. But I doubt it. You can't disguise a roofie in classic, rich bourbon—another one of Uncle Conroy's pick-up lines. God, I need to get out more.

"You asked where I was headed," Vadim points out, his voice soothingly deep—stern enough to anchor my floating brain. I shiver as he drags a finger over the back of my hand, and excited goosebumps erupt. He feels electric. "'The East coast. Then onward to the south of Italy,' I said. 'For business, not pleasure, unfortunately. Have you ever been to Europe?'"

"Oh!" Had he really been speaking all this time? I try to look away and form some semblance of a conversation. "Italy? No. But I did some of my schooling in the south of France."

"Really?" He sounds so amused. The tipsy, redhead "prostitute" summered in Leon for a while. Go figure.

"My mother insisted," I add with a giggle, facing him again. "She thought it would culture me."

All it did was put me on a crash course for a quickie marriage and a one-way ticket down heartbreak lane, smack-dab in the middle of wasted potential central.

"Does thinking about it upset you?" Vadim wonders. His voice is starting to sound way too suave. Persuasive. Enough that I might begin spilling my guts rather than offer them up to any millionaire in exchange for a lesson in kink.

"You said I might have spared you the effort of looking for a companion," I murmur to distract him, kicking my legs out as I observe him again. Damn. My eyes linger over his face this time, and my next breath catches in my throat. His eyelashes go on for days, his lips alarmingly pink. Again, my brain turns to dirty, dirty things. But a part of me almost feels ashamed for putting him in that light—even in my imagination. He looks so innocent.

"For the night, yes," he says, continuing the conversation and putting my assumption to the test. A wicked grin ignites his soft features, enhancing their intensity. "I have a few agencies I prefer to choose from. I can have my records sent to you via any method you prefer. As long as you are on regular birth control and clean, I prefer not to wear a condom."

I almost choke at how blunt he is about a subject most people in my life would clutch their pearls at the horror of discussing. More than that, he makes it sound so…orderly. So business-like.

Awed, I find myself murmuring, "You do this often?"

He nods, and I'm instantly suspicious. Someone so pretty, presumably rich, and yet he hires escorts rather than troll for celebrity arm candy? I smell bullshit. He's young enough—early-thirties I'm guessing—that a desperate actress would hitch her wagon to him in a heartbeat and supply all the sex he could ever need.

Unless relationships aren't his style.

"I prefer the ease of it," he says after a moment, seemingly proving my point. "Less hassle. Less potential for any…mess. Simple and clean."

Simple. We have that desire in common. I inhale sharply, nodding in agreement. Yes, this could work… Only, there is one tiny matter that might prove to be a hitch. "What if I'm *not* a prostitute—"

"Escort," he corrects.

"Escort then." I'm amicable to the name change—it sounds so much classier.

"If you agree to my conditions, then who am I to tell the difference?"

"Conditions?" My eyes narrow. That sounds like a potential speed bump. For instance, Uncle Conroy's "conditions"—which sent him burning through six consecutive marriages—are that he enjoys threesomes, booze, and little else. Since he's one of the few millionaires I know personally, I'm hoping his proclivities don't serve as a template for the lot. "Like?"

"Hmm." He reaches out and gently pries the nearly empty whiskey glass from my hand. Then he downs the remaining sip in one go. I gape, riveted as his throat works to swallow. Meeting my gaze, he slams the glass onto the counter, resembling a cowboy throwing down a gauntlet. "Come to my room and find out for yourself."

I stop breathing. Could it truly be so easy? A sexy businessman on my very first attempt?

Don't look a gift horse in the mouth, Uncle Conroy would warn. *Take your shot, girl. Luck doesn't strike twice.*

"Where to?" I murmur, rising to my feet.

His eyes widen—have I caught him off guard? Perhaps not. Already, a beautiful, mischievous expression erases anything else. He cocks his head and stands, offering his hand to me. "To a diversion," he says. "But first things first…"

He pulls a cell phone from his pocket, and with a series of swipes, he brings up a screen that he tilts for my inspection. It takes me a second to interpret what I see—medical records, digitized for easy access. In crisp, clinical jargon, they proclaim him to have a clean bill of health.

"Oh!" I reach into my purse and withdraw a folded slip of my own dated, printed records, drawn up by my PCP just last week, along with a copy of my birth control injection administration. He looks them over and nods.

"Shall we?" Even as he smiles that charming grin, I sense a warning in his words—that of a firm boundary being drawn between us.

He's offering up a diversion. Nothing more.

And nothing less.

CHAPTER THREE

The rest of the Six turns out to be even fancier than the lounge—not that I manage to take in much of it, considering that I can barely walk in a straight line. My heels have absolutely no grip against the plush, lush carpeting of the upper floors. I flounder gracelessly. When I nearly careen into a potted plant, a stern figure captures my wrist, pulling me against his slender frame for support.

"Easy," Vadim murmurs near my ear as I melt into him, relishing his body heat. "Are you alright?"

"Better than alright," I slur with growing determination. The alcohol running through my veins just makes me more eager for whatever Mr. Pretty might have in store. With the added bonus that if I'm terrible, or if he's terrible, or if everything is terrible, I probably won't remember by the morning.

Win, gosh darn *win.*

"It's here," Vadim says, stopping before the only door lining this hallway. When we exited the elevator we turned down one of four halls. We're on the topmost floor of the hotel. The level reserved only for the crème de la crème. Rooms more expensive than most people's mortgages.

Rooms well beyond my modest target price range of *"millionaire with thousands to blow on kink."*

"Are you trying to impress me?" I giggle, patting his chest. It's surprisingly firm, and I fan my fingers over him in curiosity. Despite his slender shape, I suspect he's solid muscle underneath. "Very funny. Where are you really staying?"

I'd already scoped out the hotel layout before infiltrating the lounge. So I know for a fact that the business and executive suites are between the tenth and thirtieth floors.

This floor sports just four suites, all exceedingly exclusive. Visiting princes and dignitaries' level of exclusive.

"Here." Vadim shoots me an odd look while reaching into the breast pocket of his jacket. He withdraws a silver key card and swipes it through the reader beside the sleek, modern door.

And it opens.

"My, oh my." I cover my mouth with my hand as I stagger forward, too curious to pretend to be unimpressed by luxury—I'd read in an online guide that to snag a rich guy's interest, pretending to be unfazed by his wealth is a must. Though Uncle Conroy seems to enjoy any pretty woman he can woo with a Rolex, so to each their own. "You must be quite the businessman to afford this. Don't tell me I'm in the presence of a millionaire."

I have the impression that Vadim intentionally stands back, allowing me to lead the way inside.

"Billionaire, perhaps," he says with a charming laugh that obscures if he's telling the truth or not. I hear the door close behind us, and his footsteps echo, advancing. "Please pardon the mess," he murmurs near the nape of my neck.

It's decided. He is officially sexy. Sexy in both appearance and in his mannerisms. The mess he's referring to seems to be a single black leather briefcase left open in the entryway of what appears to be a branching suite, complete with a spiral staircase leading to an upper level.

"Holy beans," I mutter, craning my neck back to take in the vaulted ceilings and modern architecture. "Do you always stay in the most expensive suite when you're just 'passing through' town?"

He laughs again, and my skin tingles at the sound. Actually tingles. Either that, or I am beyond tipsy and inching into drunken mess territory. Whatever, I'll worry about the consequences later.

"I have a standing reservation for convenience's sake," he says, as though it's completely normal to book a hotel room for a few hours. Could he be lying to impress me? Most likely.

Do I care?

No.

"I bet the bed is huge," I suspect, flicking my gaze toward the staircase. I slink over to it and palm the railing, feeling ten times braver than I had just minutes ago. I look over to find Vadim watching me, his dark eyes unreadable.

"Do you prefer missionary?" he inquires.

I turn away as my cheeks burn. *Stop it, Tiffy.* I'm no longer the repressed prude, but an unleashed sex kitten. For good measure, I pinch myself on the wrist.

"You know what, I've been dying to try something new," I purr, whirling around to face him. "I'm sure you have tons of experience to draw from."

That makes him smile one of those secretive grins. "I may…"

"Like?" I shed my coat as I wait for his response. It's warm in here. Too warm. Sweat is already misting over my skin, and the faux fur clings to my fingers as I set it aside.

Vadim is still standing, watching me.

"I'll let you set the pace," he says dismissively. I frown only to lose my train of thought as he runs a finger along his collar, loosening it. He's even pretty underneath the tailored fabric—his chest gleams like marble, hairless—but there's a flaw so glaring I sway at the sight. A jagged scar claims the left side of his throat, clawing down to his shoulder. With his collar done up, I'd missed it before.

"What happened?" I blurt out.

His eyes flicker, suddenly icy. "A minor accident." A deliberate note in his voice conveys a chilling bit of doublespeak—*so don't concern yourself.*

Fair enough.

Shaking my head, I refocus on the rest of him and try to recall his first directive. Set the pace.

Okay. Meeting his gaze, I attempt to advance toward him, slow and steadily like I've seen women do in pornos. But those women weren't drunk, most of them weren't wearing stilettos, and their costars weren't fully clothed, observing their every single move.

I stagger, and he practically teleports to my side, just in time to grab my arm, righting my balance before I can fall.

"I'm beginning to wonder if I might be taking advantage of you, Ms. Connors," he says, sounding annoyingly serious.

I giggle—one of those stupid, tattered drunk-girl giggles. Oh, dear, it's happened again. Well, it's too late to back down now.

"I'm fine," I insist. "In fact…"

Grab the world by the balls, Uncle Conroy would say.

So I drop to my knees and fumble for the fly of his slacks. The first thing I notice is how luxurious the fabric feels—very expensive. My second realization is how he stiffens. His body tenses beneath me, and I jump back as if burned.

"It's alright," he snaps, but irritation taints his voice like clouds obscuring a dazzling sun. Sudden and alarming.

"Sorry," I murmur, peeking up at him. "I just really want to see your—" I have to physically bite back the word "manhood"—my mother's term drilled into me since childhood. This moment calls for something dirtier. "Cock," I say instead, loving how filthy it sounds. "I really want to see your cock."

His expression shifts, neutral once again. I probably caught him off guard by how sloppy I am, and I make a concerted effort to gently brush the fastenings of his pants.

"Can I?"

"You may," he says, playful instead of serious.

I bite my lip as I work at a delicate silver clasp. With some finagling, I get it open and tug the waistband down his hips. Solidly cut muscle greets me, and I inhale in appreciation. He is *built*—as if chiseled from stone. I could cut myself on the ridges of his hips and defined thighs. But again, something detracts from the otherwise perfection.

"Are you hurt?" I ask, fingering a small, white patch placed on his abdomen, right over his hip. A thin, clear tube snakes from it, apparently connected to a rectangular device, roughly the size of a deck of cards that he withdraws from his pocket.

"Oh," I say, recognizing the device for what it is—an insulin pump. "You have diabetes?"

One of the little girls at my church had a pump, though far less high-tech than his seems to be. As I watch, he removes the patch, taking out the cannula as well. A frown tugs on his mouth as he turns and sets the device on an end table. Annoyance?

"Cold feet?" he wonders as I hesitate.

I blink, and my brain switches instantly back to sex. "I'm anything but cold," I murmur, returning my eyes to the prize—a pair of black boxers is the only remaining thing shielding him from me now. "No… I just want to savor this moment for a sec."

Impulsively reckless or otherwise, this is *it*—my moment. My first time ever sticking to a plan—no matter how outlandish—and seeing it through simply because I wanted to.

It feels damn good. Too good.

Everything is falling into place so perfectly. Usually, that only heralds bad news. Either I passed out in the lounge, and this is all a vivid hallucination, or something bad is on the horizon to dampen this moment. Either way…

I don't want to turn back.

Vadim stands utterly still as I work my fingers beneath the waistband of his boxers and tug. The moment I see all of him in full, stark glory, disappointment crashes through me so painfully I groan out loud.

This definitely is a dream.

"Something wrong?" he wonders, still so damn unaffected. Amused, even. "I must admit I'm rarely met with this reaction by the opposite sex. Though sometimes shock is expected."

"I'm sorry," I say earnestly. "I… I've just never seen a beautiful cock before."

And I've seen a lot of them. In porn, obviously, but still. Those enormous, suspiciously always erect penises were at the high end of my wildest expectations for what endowments I might discover along my new sexual adventure. But for the most part, I've kept my hopes grounded at least in the "better than Jim" range. Not too stubby, not too short, and way more willing to be placed in my mouth.

Vadim takes those mild expectations and crushes them.

"Beautiful?" Something in his tone makes me glance away with difficulty from his hips to his face. A fleeting expression shapes his features, resembling anger more than appreciation. He purses his lips a heartbeat later as if to disguise the reaction. "I'd love for you to explain, pretty girl."

My brain spins at the heated way he says that nickname. His voice drops to a lower octave, enhancing the mysterious notes of his accent. It. Is. Beyond. Sexy.

My eyelids flutter as I settle onto my knees and approach him with a single outstretched finger. When he doesn't recoil, I brush the uppermost edge of the thatch of dark curls shielding the main prize like some glorious curtain.

"It's so long," I say huskily, surprised that my voice actually sounds sexy this time. Not faked. "And…perfect," I add, inching a fraction lower. "And *pierced*."

A metal barbell goes right through the crown, topped on either end by a round bead *just* large enough to seem more tempting than intimidating. It's so deliciously sinful. So kinky.

I almost can't handle it.

"A modified Prince Albert," he explains in response to my unanswered question. "And no, it won't hurt you. That seems to be commonly asked in this situation."

By pansy fools, I decide. My only driving thought is curiosity as to how he'll feel inside me. "I've thought about getting pierced before," I tell him absently—a secret I've never spilled to anyone. Ever. "It's so pretty."

This is the extent of my vocabulary at this moment. Because all I really want to do is taste him. Part my lips around him. See how deep down I can let him go. Things I have never thought about a bodily appendage before—not even Jim's.

My eyelids get heavy, and I lick my lower lip, mulling over an angle of attack.

"I wonder what you taste like," I whisper, and I swear I see him jerk, a web of veins becoming more pronounced throughout his length. The reaction sends up a ping of alarm—does he not want me to suck him off?

"Up." He crooks a finger beneath my nose, startling me with the authority in his voice. My gaze darts to him, and I nearly sigh in relief when I catch that slow, lazy grin shaping his mouth. Not anger this time. "I've shown you mine," he explains. "Now you show me yours."

"Oh!" My brain switches gears, happily turning to something that might excite me almost as much as fellating him. Exhibiting myself for him. I lurch to my feet so quickly that I trip, and he has to grip my waist to steady me.

"Easy does it." His voice… It's so pretty when heard up close. His baritone inspires shivers that dance down my spine and shimmy in my belly. So very nice. I lean against him, straining on tiptoe to bring my nose near the crook of his shoulder. He stiffens again, but lets me inhale a whiff of him.

And it's like someone lights a match right between my legs. A noise rips from me I've never heard myself make before, and I wiggle free from him just enough to tug at the skirt of my dress.

"Allow me." He spins me around and finds the zipper nestled within my freshly blown-out hair. One tug and the fabric gives enough for me to scramble from it. I barely get my arm free of a single spaghetti-strap sleeve when a sudden tension on my hair makes me stiffen, my lips parting, spine arched. He's grabbed a handful, it seems, using his grasp to control my movements.

Like some sexy sort of leash.

"Stop," he commands in a voice so rasping my bones quiver as if made of jelly. "Allow me."

With effort, I force my hands to my side, painfully aware of his presence. My lungs ache, infected by his heady scent. His fingers are so, so soft, tracing a path from my shoulder, down the center of my back to find the zipper again.

"You have beautiful skin," he praises, sounding surprised by the fact. But his fingers brush a raised scar along my lower back, and I'm the one cringing from him this time.

"Beautiful? I've just had amazing surgeons," I insist. "It's from a boating accident and was nowhere near as painful as it looks."

But that's a dangerous topic, far too serious for my brain to comprehend.

"I have even better tits," I tell him, jutting my chest. "Not surgically enhanced, mind you."

He chuckles, and I relax into him again. Taking the hint, he slips his fingers beneath the fabric of my dress, discovering the secret that I'm not wearing a bra underneath. Or underwear.

A devious idea sneaks into my brain, and I'm too reckless to resist. As my dress falls low enough to expose the top of my butt, I inch into him just a fraction. Enough to catch his startled grunt.

"Again, I'm waffling on whether or not you truly are an escort," he grates. Gosh, I love the sound of his voice. It's like music. Sexy, disorienting music so unique it transcends any genre. "It seems you've come more than prepared."

"I'm just super horny," I confess, my breaths quickening. Something about him inspires honesty from me I'd never explore around anyone else. "Super *super* horny."

The sexy voice is back, practically vibrating from my throat. His slow-moving fingers finally reach my belly, and I can no longer be patient.

"I'd love for you to touch me," I whisper, grinding on him more. The pathetic amount of friction is like gasoline to my sex-starved brain. I want more. More more more.

"And yet another strike in the 'not an escort' column," he muses. "You, pretty girl, are far too disobedient."

"Disobedient." I toy with the word between my tongue and giggle at how silly it sounds—considering that the opposite term had been my sole defining attribute for the better part of the past decade. The good obedient housewife. Good, obedient Tiffy. Subservient, oh so likable and so depressed, she contemplated suicide at least once per week—screw obedience.

"I've upset you." Vadim snatches on my hips, turning me to face him. His dark eyes skim over me, but a part of me buzzes faintly in alarm. His expression doesn't match the concern in his voice one damn bit. He looks too…excited. Like discovering my ticks is a fun, thrilling game.

So I rake my fingers down the front of his chest and lower my gaze to his cock. It's slightly more erect, thicker than before, those veins even more pronounced. He's aroused by this. Giddy triumph surges straight to my brain. I'd clap my hands if they weren't too busy relishing the feel of him. So sturdy. So very solid.

"I want you to finger me, please," I tell him, barely able to keep my eyes open. "Pretty please. I've been dying for it."

Another low, amused chuckle. I'm entertaining him. But a part of me loves the thrill of being on display—no cares given.

"Touch me," I beg, taking it a step further. "I bet your fingers feel amazing."

"Show me how, pretty girl." He shoves me back, and I have no chance in hell of preventing the fall. Luckily, I land on something soft that conforms to my shape—a leather couch. With enviable grace, Vadim steps forward, forcing my legs to part to give him room. With him looming above me, I feel smaller than ever. Something delicate at his mercy. Or disposal.

"Show me," he repeats, grabbing my wrist.

I gasp as he guides my hand between my legs and my thighs part on command. Years of both secret and more recently, regular masturbation have made me an expert at it. With the right mood and setting, I can get myself off in no time flat. In some ways, it's become a chore. Flick, flick. Twist, twist. Boom, there goes Tiffy.

But this...

Having a beautiful man's dark, beautiful eyes track my every move is an experience unto itself. Already soaked, my folds part easily with one brush of my forefinger. But the sensation—it's *lightning*. My head rears back as my teeth skewer my lower lip, trapping a moan inside.

A new record. No amount of porno or dirty reading material has ever gotten me this close, this fast. My fingers still, and I'm almost terrified to move. How pathetic would it be to get myself off so quickly?

But if anything, Vadim doesn't look disappointed. His eyes gleam as I part my legs and risk slipping one finger inside me. My body convulses as nerves explode despite my attempts to stave off the pleasure. But I fight the spasms just to watch him.

Holy hell. No man should be able to look like this. Aloof, and yet at the same time ravenous. Like a vulture who knows that the antelope writhing in agony before him is almost ready to feast upon. Almost.

He just needs to let it die first.

"Please touch me." I'm whining as I inch my finger deeper inside me while stroking my clit with my thumb. Usually, it takes a few good strokes to get me going. Now? "Oh gosh—"

Vadim moves with a calculated focus. One of his hands grabs my thigh, wrenching it higher as he palms his cock with the other. It's a sight unlike any other—his piercing glows, electric amid the swollen crown. No porno could ever compare to this, watching him angle himself against me.

My eyes roll as he slams forward, thrusting inside me with no preamble.

And I nearly come off the couch. He's so big. One thrust takes him deep, so deep. I cry out as my body grips him so hard I swear I can feel the outline of each one of those pulsating veins —every curve of his piercing.

And it feels beyond good.

My brain boils more with every thrust. Any semblance of coherence my thoughts possessed dissolves. I claw at him, nails drawn, urging him deeper, harder—to give me everything.

But when glimpsed through my heavy eyelids, he looks more determined than ever. Like a doctor carefully doling out an allotment of medicine. Just enough to do the trick.

But never enough to overload.

Never enough to lose control.

I'm aware of it—the boundary he maintains even as I tremble around him, gasping for breath. How he grips the back of the couch as if to maintain the same, consistent rhythm as he thickens inside me, demanding more…

That he denies himself of claiming.

And when he growls through his own release, he doesn't throw his head back in triumph. Instead, he grits his teeth, cutting off the noise. Closes his eyes, cutting *me* off.

"N-No!" I arch into him, letting my body grip him so ravenously we both cry out. "I want to see you. Please…"

His eyes reopen, but they're dark. Detached. Disconnected.

He withdraws abruptly, letting me slump against the couch. A lazy smile shapes his lips before panic can even set in fully—but it persists, nonetheless. This horrible sense that I've done something wrong. Offended him somehow.

Or that for him, real no-holds-barred pleasure was never part of the deal. As if reading my mind, he steps forward, his gaze softer. But his frown persists, ruining the façade he puts up. I'm five seconds from salvaging my pride and leaving altogether when he cups my jaw, tilting my head back to easily meet his gaze.

"Beautiful," he says, his voice deep.

And I let my brain turn off, ignoring those tiny warning signs urging me to run.

CHAPTER FOUR

Somehow, we wind up on the floor with me on top of him, his hands on my waist. I marvel at the beauty of his body, feeling up whatever parts of him I can reach. Even his scar. Despite its jagged appearance, the skin feels surprisingly soft to the touch—like silk.

"You're so pretty," I tell him, barely able to feel my tongue.

He found another bottle of wine from somewhere, and it tastes even better than what they served downstairs. Dangerously sweet, enough that I'm already on my second glass.

You're a mess, Tiffy, a part of me scolds. But being a mess is surprisingly fun. Alcohol enhances every sensation to the nth degree. I giggle, relishing the tingling, tightening feel as my body recovers. But Vadim is watching me, eerily alert. Again, I can't shake this tiny voice warning me that he's almost too alert. I don't remember seeing him drink though he lazily pours more into my glass without bothering to sit up.

Whatever. I'll worry about that later.

"Tell me something," I slur to distract from the feeling. "Something you've never told anyone ever." When his brows furrow skeptically, I stroke my finger along his chin and add, "I can assure you that there is a fifty percent chance I won't remember any of this by tomorrow."

Another dizzying chuckle escapes him. Gosh, he could drug someone on his voice alone. "Only fifty? I hate to break it to you, Tiffany, but you are thoroughly sloshed."

I concede to that assumption with a nod. "Yeah. Which makes show and tell even funner!"

"Why don't you start?" he suggests. Extending his finger, he tucks a stray curl behind my ear, lingering near the lobe.

"Okay…" I suck in a breath and exhale it in an involuntary giggle that ruins the gravity of this moment. Here goes nothing. "I *did* scope you out on purpose," I confess. "I'm not a prostitute —but I do want something from you."

His eyes practically glow, smug. As if he knew as much all along. "Money?" he guesses. "Clout? Protection from an abusive spouse that has you on the run?"

I snicker and raise my hand to tick off each debunked assumption one by one. "First, the abusive spouse is long since divorced. Second, I have all the money I need. And clout—" I burst into cackling laughter and lose track of which finger I was on. "What does that even mean?"

"Power," he says seriously. "Men in my position possess plenty of power. Some seek to manipulate it for themselves."

"Hmm." I hum, brushing my lips along his throat. His scar is surprisingly the softest part of him, and I linger over the contours of it, daring to sneak a taste with a flick of my tongue.

"I *love* how power sounds when you say it. Your voice is so sexy—"

"You are overly affectionate when you're drunk." I frown at the obvious distaste in his voice, but when I scan his expression, I don't find anything but a humored smirk. He's so good at hiding himself.

I should be worried about that, I think.

Or I can take another sip of wine. Smacking my lips, I set my glass down and nearly knock it over.

"I *am* drunk," I confess, sadly. "The cat is out of the bag. Such a poor little pussy. It hasn't been out in ages—"

"So, what was it you wanted from me?"

I shiver, easily distracted. His breath even smells nice, deliciously warm, tinged with whiskey. "I was hoping you were part of a sex club," I confess against his chest. "Like, the really debauched, really exclusive kind with pillories and such. Super taboo, kinky sex. The kind only rich people can have in utter confidentiality."

Something weird happens. His face… It's like he knew exactly what I would say down to the last period. But then drunk Tiffy mixed-up the script, catching him off guard. Even worse, irritating him. My stomach drops to the floor, and I rush to clean-up my own mess.

"I'm sorry—"

"You think you can survive in such a club?" he wonders in a tone that chills me, all ounce of humor gone.

"Maybe," I say quickly. "But I've survived seven years of boring, milk toast sex and utter misery, so I'm ready for a challenge.

Joining a place like that is on my list," I add with solemn seriousness.

"List?" He raises an eyebrow, still so tense. Edgy.

Sighing, I try to find the right words to explain. "My 'no one owns me, fuck all list.' It has five items—"

"Just five?" he counters, and I snicker. Is that amusement I detect?

Raising my hand, I start to tick them off. "Yes. Dress how I want. Fuck how I want. Live how I want. Eat what I want. And no relationships."

That last one is a new addition, but he relaxes beneath me. For whatever reason, I think I've given him the right answer. To what question? He's so mysterious—I wonder if I'll ever know.

"But I feel bad for profiling you," I add, tapping his nipple. Mentally, I try to stop myself from using the word "beautiful" to describe the dusky peak. But it is. Gosh, he's like some alternate version of Adonis come to life. "I now think you're very straight-laced," I say, treating the term as a compliment. "I don't think you belong to a kinky, Godless sex club—"

"Oh, but I do." His upper lip quirks into one of those quick, devious grins. "One of the most debauched in the country, in fact. Though I will admit that I've let my membership lapse."

"R-Really?" My eyes go bug wide, and I scramble into a sitting position, straddling his slender hips. "Do they do orgies?" I wonder, practically squealing with excitement. "Do they do bondage? BDSM? Exhibition? Gang bangs?"

Kid, meet candy store. If I somehow manage to remember this in the morning, I'll never stop speculating.

"I don't know the menu offhand," he admits. "But you never asked me what my confession might be?"

"Oh, yes!" I extend my fist toward him as a makeshift microphone. "Mr. Vadim Gorgoshev, what secrets are you hiding?"

"I'm not on my way to a business meeting," he says. That's right —he did mention leaving for a flight soon.

I flutter my eyelashes. "So, where are you going?"

"My brother is throwing a party." His tone makes it sound about as appealing as an execution mixed with a root canal.

"I take it you two don't get along?"

His lips twitch into a sly grin. "One could say that."

"So why go?"

He seems to be pondering that exact question. Whatever answer he decides on, he doesn't say out loud.

"Well, at least you got to have some fun before you leave." I shift, shamelessly rubbing my nipples against his chest, loving the sensation that sparks in response.

"Fun?" He raises an eyebrow. "You aren't going to stroke my ego and tell me it was the most mind-blowing fucking you've ever experienced? All in the hopes of weaseling an invitation to the club out of me, of course."

"It was definitely the best I've ever been fucked." My wistful tone could convince even a blind man that I'm not lying. "But... You held back." I make my finger dance down his abdomen, able to sense the subtle tensing of his body. He maintains that invisible wall between us, even as we lie drunk on the floor, utterly naked.

"It's fine, though. I'm sure you have some kind of control freak mental hang-up that makes it hard to let loose. I get it. God knows I do. It's probably for the best."

Mindless, emotionally-charged sex is a unicorn I'm better off not chasing.

"You gave me what I wanted, so thank you very, very much…" I trail off as I finally notice his expression. Dark eyes narrowed, lips pursed in contemplation. I've annoyed him again.

"I mean it," I insist. "It was amazing—"

"Come with me," he says.

My poor, drunk brain can't compute a response. All I can think to say is, "Where?"

The grin returns, playfully stern. "To the party, beautiful."

I smile inwardly at the new nickname. An upgrade from pretty. Then smart, good-girl Tiffany manages to get a stranglehold on lusty-Tiffy just long enough for me to ask, "You want me to meet your family?"

It sounds suspicious. *Very* suspicious when paired with the fact that I can no longer get a solid read on him. His teasing grin could hide a million ulterior motives.

But when his fingers find a lock of my hair and toy with it, I forget a teensy bit of the paranoia.

"It's just a party," he says—though were someone to tell that to my mother about one of her carefully crafted soirees, she just might reach for a kitchen knife with murderous intent. Something in his tone robs all sentimentality from the term, at least in this instance.

"Admittedly, it's in another city, but I'm willing to fly you there and arrange for your transportation back, all at no expense to you."

"Could you even get a ticket this late? You're leaving in…" I glance at a clock hanging on the wall, and a panicked bit of despair leeches into my tone. "Roughly one hour."

So darn soon. Thus ends Tiffy's first foray into sexual exploration. And darn was it fun.

"Come with me," Vadim insists. "It's a private plane, so no ticket required. We'll get in by the morning. You can have the day to shop. The party is in the evening, and you can be on a flight back before the night ends. And," he adds, presumably to present the tempting carrot to my desperate mule. "In exchange, I'll grant you an exclusive membership to my club. Granted, it's in Fair Haven, on the East coast, so you will have to find your own way back, should you decide to utilize it."

I pout and roll off him to contemplate my options. He's managed to present a multitude of both tempting and grounding proposals in one go, all neatly wrapped with a bow.

A whirlwind day to distract from having to dip my toe in the businessman waters again.

A guaranteed trip back.

A membership to a bona fide sex club.

And, a shopping trip thrown in, presumably all-expenses paid.

But the part I find surprisingly bracing is his casual acknowledgment that we're done after that. No contact, and should I one day wander into his sex club, it will be on my own dime and time.

Fair enough.

"Will we have sex again?" I wonder. I'm shocked by how much I'm hoping for a yes. A chance to experience him again and give my fellatio skills another go. A chance to see what might lurk beneath his invisible mask.

"No," he says, dashing my hopes. "I don't mean to offend you, but I don't think you're my type. I hope I didn't give you the wrong impression."

I wince. His rejection hurts more than it should, though it certainly explains a lot. His amusement. The invisible wall. The fact that he stopped short of handcuffing me just to keep me off his cock. There certainly is a bit of irony to it, though. I started this night uninterested, only now I can't get his smirk out of my head. Or those eyes. Or his scent...

Leaving now would be the smart, responsible thing to do.

"What would my shopping budget be?" I ask him instead.

He chuckles. "The sky is the limit."

Somehow, I keep my eyes from bugging out. Humming in contemplation, I tap my chin, thinking it over. "Tempting, tempting..."

"But you still aren't sold?" He rolls over and captures my chin, making me face him. Eyes glittering like coals, he takes me in from my hair all the way down to my still curling toes. "What can I do to seal the deal?"

I sigh, suddenly exhausted. The alcohol is finally taking its toll on my brain, dulling my senses and making me sluggish. Finding the strength to answer him at all is a challenge, but one I feel obligated to accept. "Fine. Tell me what about me changed your mind."

Because he *had* been interested. I could tell from the way he looked at me in the bar—that quick, fleeting glance when I started to walk away.

"You don't like redheads? My tits are too small?" I fondle said tits morosely. "I can handle it. Promise." I lift my pinky in solemn solidarity.

"Don't take it personally," he scolds while propping his chin on his fist. The elevated position allows him to stare down on me, unreadable as my eyelids grow heavier by the second. "Personal preference is no insult."

"I know that." I'm pouting, but I'm far too gone to care. "Still want to hear it, though."

"You're too unpredictable," he says. "I prefer my trysts to be…uncomplicated."

"That's it?" I roll my eyes, and they wind up closing for good. I'm too exhausted to open them again. "Talk about a shitty reason."

"Oh?"

"Yes," I snap, suddenly irritated, though the word comes out a slurred mixture between a whine and sigh. "No one *likes* the predictable. It's just that some men can't handle not controlling everything from their lifestyle, to when they come. I'm talking from experience," I add, in case he decides to challenge me.

But he doesn't.

Confusion spurs me to muster up just enough strength to crack open one eye to observe him.

And I gasp. He's angry. Truly, unashamedly angry. Fire crackles through his eyes, gathering in the corners of that supple mouth. I suck in a breath, recoiling.

"I don't think you'd like how I handle the unpredictable," he warns. My heart throbs in the face of it, my nerves zapping.

It's the sexiest, most alarming thing I've ever seen.

And it's the sight that haunts me as I finally pass out.

CHAPTER FIVE

I groan, torn between writhing in agony and regretting the life choices that led me to this point. This point being lying on an unfamiliar bed, craving Tylenol with every fiber of my being, and cursing the effects of alcohol to hell and back.

The fact that I don't know where I am or how I got here can be addressed later.

At the moment, all I can do is peel my eyes open and scan my surroundings for any hint of immediate danger—and, or, a bathroom. *Bingo!* In a blurred sea of navy blue walls and blinding windows, I spot an open door that looks promising enough.

Somehow, I stagger to my feet, feeling out for whatever I can find to steady my balance. When my bare toes finally leave plush carpeting for what feels like cold tile, I sink to my knees and crawl toward a porcelain basin that has never looked so beautiful before.

From my murky teenage recollections, I remember that the easiest way for me to cure a hangover has been to vomit. Purge whatever is left in my system and then crawl into a steaming hot shower until the life returns to my limbs.

The shower in this bathroom is a huge, imposing rectangle of glass. An LED panel seems to control it but appears to need the wisdom of an electronics engineer to utilize it. Groaning, I press buttons and curse until water gushes in from about ten thousand showerheads. It's freezing cold, and I scream as the spray hits me.

But it will do.

Time to collect yourself, Tiffy, the stern, good-girl part of me warns, fully resurrected. *Try to remember what happened. How big of a mess do you need to salvage this time?*

Hmm… Well, I vaguely remember scoping out someone handsome at the bar. Very handsome, the tingle in my belly tells me. But I can't escape the sense that something was wrong with him. So wrong that he's no longer an option—not that I was looking for anything long-term anyway.

We went to his room, I think.

And then… We had sex. Which explains why my pussy is throbbing like hell, and my lips feel swollen. We had very good, very impersonal sex. Then we talked for what felt like hours, and I agreed to come with him…somewhere.

Gosh, what was his name? Gorgo? Vlad…*Vadim.*

And he, apparently, is nowhere to be found. Nice.

"You brought it on yourself, Tiffy," I scold myself out loud. My teeth are chattering, and once I feel coherent enough to form a more solid thought other than—*holy crap what have I done*—I fiddle with the panel until the water turns off, and then I crawl out of the stall.

The bathroom itself is enormous. White marble creates a crisp, clean color scheme that makes me feel like something dirty and unwanted that slithered in through the drain. I'm still wearing my beautiful, now ruined "sexual revolution dress," though I don't know where the faux fur jacket is, or my shoes for that matter.

Using the wall for balance, I manage to wrap a towel around myself and reenter the room I woke up in.

Make that, the *executive suite* I woke up in. A massive bed dominates the center of a sleek, modern room composed of navy walls interspersed with floor to ceiling windows that display a skyscraper laden view of a city. A vast, industrial city a world apart from sleepy Main Oaks, California.

Thrown over a leather armchair in the corner of the room is my jacket, with my shoes neatly placed on the floor nearby. The place apparently comes with its own soundtrack as well—a persistent, high-pitched ringing…

Oh. I spot a silver phone on a glass end table near the bed and warily approach it. "H-Hello?" I whisper after bringing the receiver to my ear.

"You're awake," a musically accented voice remarks. "Good. You slept in later than expected. You have only three hours to find something to wear. Our budget will remain as discussed."

"B-Budget?" I frown, rubbing my forehead. "I'm sorry…who is this?"

A low, devious chuckle serves to kick start my memory. *Vadim.*

"I believe you should avoid mixing your liquor with wine from now on, Ms. Connors," he says, playing with the syllables in my name. "I'll be around to pick you up at six. In the meantime, I've informed the hotel to allow you unlimited use of a town car and driver. Feel free to shop where you like. The driver has a card for you to use. My only stipulation is that you find something sexy. The more revealing, the better."

"Sexy?" My breathing hitches as I take the card as though it's made of glass. Memories are starting to come back to me, one in particular that still smarts. "I thought you said we weren't going to have sex."

"We aren't," he states matter of factly. "But my brother surrounds himself with a certain type of crowd. I don't want you to stand out."

Fair enough. "Where are you?" I wonder, gazing from the window. "Where are *we*?"

"Fair Haven," he says as though I asked him what color the sky was. "As for where I am, I had some business to see to. Until tonight. Oh, and if you need to change your dress, I arranged to have an outfit bought for you. It's in the closet."

He hangs up, leaving my brain reeling. Frowning, I stumble around the room until I find a sliding wooden door that conceals a walk-in closet. Inside, on a single hanger hangs a lone white sundress. It's not too shabby, though a bit conservative for my tastes. My new tastes anyway.

I slip it on and wrestle some semblance of humanity into my hair and splash water onto my face. When I reach the hotel lobby, I'm surprised to find an aura that feels more exclusive than the Six. Gold walls and polished black floors convey decadent luxury. A concierge even comes to meet me right at the elevator.

"You must be Ms. Connors," he says warmly. "William is already bringing the car around. Can I get you anything while you wait? Coffee? Tea? A glass of wine, perhaps?"

Still suffering from my current hangover, I nearly choke. "N-No thanks."

He ushers me into a private booth as I wait, and when the driver arrives, he professes his intent to wait for me as long as required.

A smile tugs on my mouth for the first time as I enter the back of a sleek silver vehicle.

This might be fun.

CURSING, I attempt to swipe my room key through the reader while juggling an armful of shopping bags. Finally, success! I kick open the door and hop inside, only to scream as my eyes settle over a figure glowering in the center of the sprawling suite.

"I told you six," Vadim snaps. He's already dressed in a sleek ebony suit, tailored to perfection. His dark curls conform to his skull, slightly mussed. Capping off the look is a blood-red tie that betrays a hint of the daring nature I've come to suspect he regularly suppresses. "We're going to be late…"

He trails off when he notices the army of bags at my disposal.

"Hear me out," I plead, holding up my hands in a gesture of surrender. "I couldn't decide what to wear. And then traffic was hell. And…" I fish through my bags and brandish a luxuriously wrapped package in triumph. "I got your brother a gift. And his wife, if he has one." I wield a second gift in my opposite hand and smile as sweetly as I physically can.

"He has a fiancée," Vadim grunts, still surly.

So I resort to plan B and start to shimmy out of my dress. "Don't hate me until you see the options," I say in a rush. "Option one —" I snatch a garment from a black bag betraying the name of a designer I used to worship back when I had the lack of brains and excess funds to spend on clothing. A deep shade of navy, the slim-fitting cocktail dress sets off the red in my hair and conforms to my shape. Sexy, but modestly so.

"No," Vadim says, observing me with a frown. "It is a party, not a church service."

"Ah." So maybe life with Jim is harder to shake than I thought? No matter. Skipping to another bag, I dig out my second option.

"No," he growls before I can even pull it on—a black, moderately more revealing mini dress.

"Okay. Big guns, then. Now when you said sexy, I hope you meant…stripper. Because that is this dress." I reach for my final option, and his eyes narrow thoughtfully. When it isn't met with instant rejection, I tug it on, wrenching the tiny frock down over my hips.

It's a *not-safe-for-work-fuck-me* dress in Jessica Rabbit scarlet with her flair for the daring. A bold, plunging neckline reveals the globes of both my breasts, and the view extends almost to my navel. The back is equally low cut, but given the quality of the fabric, it's admittedly more high-class escort than stripper.

"This will do," Vadim says. He lunges forward and grabs my wrist, dragging me from the room before I can even get my bearings.

"W-Wait—"

"We're late," he growls. He must not have been kidding about things being tense between him and his brother. I only manage to slip on my heels and grab the two presents before I find myself tugged into the elevator, dragged from the hotel, and promptly shoved within a scarlet sports car waiting out front.

Vadim takes the wheel, still scowling.

I feel drawn to tap his shoulder once, my frown apologetic. "I'm sorry," I say as he pulls into traffic. "I'm terrible with time management. Jim—I mean… Some people used to say I'd miss the rapture because I'd just have to go back and grab the perfect tube of lipstick to wear through the holy gates."

He doesn't laugh.

I try another tack. "Do you live here in Fair Haven?"

Still no answer.

Sighing, I sit back in my seat and wring my fingers together. "If you're angry with me, you might as well just yell about it. Otherwise, I'll talk and talk to fill the silence. I can't stand it to be honest. I would rather be boiled alive than—"

"So it wasn't the wine that made you so talkative." His tone is so cutting, I wince.

"*Touché,* Mr. Gorgoshev. I… Are you okay?"

He's shivering, his body vibrating over the seat. His teeth chatter, but his eyes are narrowed and focused.

I fumble with the dials on the console until the heat kicks on.

"Maybe I should check for a fever—"

"I'd prefer it if you stopped talking, please," he says, still devastatingly polite.

I fall silent, stung for reasons I can't name. For all of his surliness, I hate the fact that I might have disappointed him.

It isn't long before we pull up before what I assume is the entrance to a private stretch of property along a waterfront, just beyond the city limits. Without a word of warning to me, Vadim strikes the button that lowers the window on his end.

"I was *invited*," he says, but his voice is sharper than the low, delicious hum I'm used to. It's cold, and the contrast has me sitting straighter in my seat. He's speaking to a man who came seemingly from nowhere, dressed in black to blend in with the shadowed surroundings. An earpiece is attached to his left ear, which he fingers while murmuring something too softly for me to make out. Then he nods us forward.

"You can go."

A smug, icy expression dominates Vadim's features, exaggerating the harsher lines of his face and diminishing the softness. I'm tempted to try probing him again—something more than my tardiness has to be bothering him—but then I spy the structure looming before us at the end of a long driveway, and I promptly lose my train of thought.

"Holy crap, it's beautiful," I murmur.

The house is far from the gaudy, showy properties I grew up in and among. The architecture alone conveys wealth, but subtly. Warm light emanating from within highlights the stone base with rustic accents of wood and beautiful, arched windows displaying a snippet of the home's interior where several people mill about a wide, spacious room.

Excitement sneaks in, nibbling away at any lingering doubt. While navigating a surly millionaire—sorry, supposed *billionaire*

—is a new experience, if there's one thing I know, it's parties. Juggling the presents in both hands, I watch Vadim exit the car, and I let loose a relieved sigh as he crosses to my end and opens the door for me.

"I'll be good, I promise," I tell him with a smile.

But he isn't even looking in my direction. He eyes the house up ahead as though it's a battlefield. One he's willing to dominate at all costs.

A shiver of unease runs through me as I follow him, finding my balance in my new—and higher—stilettos. A paved stone path leads to a wide porch at the front of the house. We've barely managed to mount the first step when the door flies open so brutally it slams into the wall and ricochets off with a sound like a gunshot.

Startled, I jump and nearly trip off the steps entirely, but Vadim's hand captures my hip, righting my balance.

"You dare come here?" a man demands, his voice heavily accented and booming like thunder. I have to crane my neck back to take him in; he's so tall. So huge. A wall of muscle, he nearly consumes the entire doorway, barely leaving space for the startled people standing behind him. He radiates fury, his expression so cold I'm instantly chilled and find myself inching closer to Vadim.

Not that he's a beacon of warmth at the moment—he's trembling even more than before.

"Let him in, Maxim," a softer, less stern voice commands from within the house. A British accent plays with the speaker's pronunciation, making every word sound stern yet polite. "Tell me, is causing a scene really worth it? Now? Here?"

Maxim, presumably the big man, finally stands aside. Light from inside the house spills out, illuminating the long blond hair streaming down his shoulders. Angular features craft a handsome, if stern, face, and his eyes are so dark, they seem to feed on the shadows.

"If it breaks the tension, I invited him," the British speaker insists. A dark-haired man steps forward, wearing a gunmetal gray suit. He's alluringly handsome, but something in his gaze makes me look away rather than ogle. Wolves are pretty too, but even I know better than to make eye contact with one.

"Come, Dima," he adds. "I'm sure you came here only to celebrate with us."

I know a warning not to piss on the couch when I hear it. Usually, said warnings are directed toward me. *Be good, Tiffy. Don't fuck this up, Tiffy. Just be fucking normal, Tiffany!*

"I'll try to be on my very best behavior," Vadim simpers. The shift in his personality is even more palpable now. I glance over to find his eyes flashing, ignited with that mischievous gleam times a million.

Uh, oh. A part of me warns. *What the hell have I stepped into?*

All I can do is follow all three men into the house where I quickly realize that—one, it's just as beautiful as the outside. Two, if sexy was the dress code, then I'm the only person who got the memo.

In addition to the three men, two women linger on the outskirts of a massive, open floor plan living room. Both wear modest and yet fashionable black gowns presumably tailored to their individual preferences. A slender brunette wears hers slightly short, but with a conservative neckline while a striking blond models a slightly longer design with fashionable sleeves. Though, strangely, she looks just as uncomfortable as I feel being here, her large eyes darting between all three men.

It doesn't take me long to realize what might be guiding their fashion choices—the presence of children. Small ones. Bigger ones. At least six in total stand scattered throughout the room. A little boy with huge brown eyes takes one look at me and scampers over to a small girl with long sandy hair. "You can see her boobies," he stage-whispers to her.

And I feel slapped. Used. My entire body tenses up with the realization that he urged me to dress this way on purpose. To cause a scene. Prove a point. It's happened before—being the girl who arrives to a party braless in a thin white T-shirt because she was stupid enough to fall for the "It's a charity wet T-shirt contest" line.

Humiliation washes over me in crippling, searing waves, and all I want to do is sink into the floor and die. Old Tiffy would have. She would have crumbled to pieces and run from this room in tears. She would have berated herself for being so stupid. So weak. She would be an easy target.

But I'm not her anymore.

Reigning in the shame takes all of five seconds. I jut out my chin into the air, square my shoulders, and plaster a charming grin on my face the likes of which would make my mother proud.

"Oh gosh, I am so sorry," I declare, laughing politely. *Haha, silly me.* "Poor Vadim tried to warn me that this dress might be a bit much, but I didn't pay him any mind." I turn to him and playfully slap him on the forearm—hard. If he notices the hostility, his expression doesn't show it. "If it isn't too much trouble, could I borrow a jacket or a shawl?"

"Here, Miss." An older gentleman steps forward and shrugs his own suit jacket from his shoulders, offering it to me.

I shimmy into it, balancing my gifts. I can sense Vadim watching me from the corner of my eye, the bastard. Smiling harder, I turn the charm up to eleven.

"You must be the brother," I exclaim, turning to the dark-haired man. It's a logical guess, considering his hair color, but when I glance at the blond man, I realize my mistake. No two creatures could possess eyes that shade by accident. "My apologies. *You* are the brother," I declare, turning to him. Smiling prettily, I extend my gift and force myself to meet his cold, piercing stare. "I'm Tiffany. Thank you so much for inviting us. We picked out something small to show our appreciation." When he doesn't take the present, I laugh nervously. Desperate for an escape, I set it down on a nearby end table instead. "And your fiancée must be..." I pivot and spot the two women again. The blond eyes me, her expression unreadable, but the brunette looks as uncomfortable as a deer in the headlights. *Bingo.*

"You must be the fiancée!" I cross to her and nearly sigh in relief when she accepts the gift.

"I'm Francesca," she says softly. Her voice lacks an accent, at least, but she's young. Really young. I do a double take of Vadim's brother, and I have to fight back the inner judgmental voice wondering just how young she truly is.

"Well, I'm so sorry we made a scene," I say, returning to Vadim's side. He's rigid, unmoving even as I grasp his hand and shamelessly dig my nails into the palm of it.

He'll pay for this later. Oh, he will so pay. But for now, I know it's better to play my part and bide my time. No one will ever make a fool of me again, out of spite or otherwise.

"So, what are we celebrating?" I ask.

The two brooding men share a look.

"An engagement," Vadim says before either one can offer up an answer themselves.

"Lovely!" I clap my hands, my smile beaming. "Congratulations!"

I swear everyone flinches.

But I take the awkward tension as a challenge. I will survive this, so help me, God.

Or I will gleefully take Vadim down with me.

CHAPTER SIX

When it comes to parties and how to play them to their fullest, there is no match for a mansion born, cotillion raised Connors socialite. I learned from the best—Genevieve Mackenzie Adalynn Connors, who operated her events with me balanced on her hip while juggling a serving tray and a hospitable smile.

She had the grace and charm required to turn any hostile gathering into a soiree so warm and welcoming; she could sow world peace if the room were big enough. Emulating her, I only manage to simmer what tensions lurk between these men to the barest minimum—and I'm nearly sweating with the effort.

Dinner is an awkward lesson in how to juggle the tersest small talk with a grin and a funny quip.

"So when is your wedding?" I ask, referring to the supposed reason for this "party."

Maxim and his fiancée share a searching glance. "Soon," he says in a tone that makes me scramble for my glass of wine. "It will be a *private* affair." His eyes slice in Vadim's direction with chilling intensity. I have a feeling he won't be getting an invite.

"What a shame," Vadim replies, his teeth bared. "I was so looking forward to witnessing the nuptials. Some might say we'd thought to never see the day you'd settle down with *one* of your women."

"I've always preferred intimate ceremonies," I blurt in a rush, parrying the incoming blow from Maxim before the man can even open his mouth. Across the table, poor Francesca's cheeks turn blood red though the children innocently chatter amongst themselves, oblivious. Thank God. "I wish I'd had a small wedding," I add wistfully. "Maybe a destination one?"

At least then, I could look back on the memories fondly. Instead, my only recollections consist of sweating in a massive gown bought on my parent's dime while being paraded before what seemed like the entire parish. That day, instead of marital bliss, my main takeaway from the experience is the memory of the pain from holding a fake smile in place for sixteen hours.

I'm so lost in the nostalgia that I barely notice the rest of the conversation has gone silent. Good. As far as social landscapes go, this one is my most challenging battlefield yet. I feel like I'm juggling knives. One wrong move, and everyone gets stabbed in the eye.

But I manage, with no assistance from the very man who brought me here.

Something happens to him in the presence of his brother. Something dark that festers within him, seeping out in cold, icy sarcasm and glittering, unreadable eyes.

It's the eyes that unnerve me the most. His wall is back in place, higher than ever. Insurmountable.

"At least you're dressed fucking decently," his brother hisses as we get through most of the first course. "Have you grown bored of crawling in the shadows, luring children away?"

The British man, Milton, lifts his hand and pinches the bridge of his nose.

"I have," Vadim replies with a manic grin. He's still shivering, more noticeably than before. I can't resist slipping my hand into his pocket, hoping to provide some warmth—but he recoils from me so violently he jolts the entire table.

"This has been lovely," he says, lurching to his feet in an enviable display of grace. "Sadly, we must be going."

"Awww!" The little girl whines from her spot near the end of the table. "You have to go now?"

"Ainsley…" Francesca cuts her gaze in the girl's direction, her tone a warning.

Undeterred, Ainsley pouts. "I wanted to show you my pony, Uncle Dima."

"Some other time," he says before taking a gallant bow.

"Wait." Milton inclines his head toward Maxim. Something wordlessly passes between the two of them. Then Milton turns to Vadim. "Dinner," he says. "Neutral territory. Next week?"

Vadim says nothing and starts from the room, leaving me to follow. At the door, I return the jacket to the older man, and by the time I leave the house, Vadim is already at the car.

With his back to me, he palms the door. "You survived." He has the nerve to sound surprised at that. Impressed.

"Fuck. You," I spit, utilizing the dirtiest word in my newfound freedom-vocabulary. When he whirls around, an eyebrow cocked in amusement; I lose any shred of restraint. Leveling him with my nastiest glare, I go off. "You used me. You dragged me here, for what? To make your brother think you disrespected him by bringing some stupid slut around his children? To his home? What the hell is wrong with you?"

"Plenty." His jaw clenches, his expression icier than ever. "You earned this, I suppose," he says, flicking something at me too quickly to catch. Thin, rectangular, and silver, it lands at my feet —some type of business card. "When you make a reservation, use my name," he states. "Otherwise, you won't be allowed entry."

I eye the card again, recognizing it for what it is. The price of my humiliation, it seems—entrance to some exclusive sex club.

"You know what? Screw you!" I flip him the finger and start down the driveway, staggering in my heels. "Do you know how you made me feel?"

"Inconvenienced?" he guesses in that cutting tone. "The feeling was mutual, I can assure you—"

"Sabotaged," I snap, whirling to face him. "Insulted. Humiliated. Hurt. I told myself a long time ago that I would never let anyone ever make me feel that way again."

Go figure. I've failed in that respect.

"Consider it practice for when you bare yourself before strangers who only want to fuck you," he suggests. "I do hope you enjoy the amenities. I hear they're quite debauched."

My cheeks flame and something inside me snaps. "Practice? Oh, trust me, I don't need any practice. After that night with you, I'm *desperate* to be ogled by someone who doesn't think he's too good to have his cock sucked."

His eyes widen and narrow in quick succession. Did I hit a sore spot? Gosh, I hope so.

"Does this get you off rather than fucking?" I wonder, gesturing around us with a harsh, cackling laugh. "Bringing me all the way across the country to what? Get under your brother's skin? Hurt some sleazy slut who had the nerve to approach you? Well, sorry to break it to you, but I'm fine, Vadim. I am more than fine!" I stroll past him and stoop for the business card, brandishing it like a hard-fought trophy. "You know what, I will go get ogled by strangers, and I'm going to enjoy every fucking minute of it! I'm going to fuck as many men as I can, too. Suck every last cock that will have me, and then..." My chest heaves, my body radiating anger, and I have to gulp down enough air just to keep going. "I'm going to compare every last one of them to yours. How they feel. How they taste. From now on, I'm going to keep a running tally of all the bastards who fuck better than Vadim Gorgoshev could ever dream. Choke on that while you're on your private plane."

Card in tow, I keep marching down the driveway, blinking rapidly. *Almost there, Tiffy,* I plead with my inner waterworks. *Just a little more. You can make it.*

"Oh, and don't think you've stranded me or that I'll be crying out on the street tonight," I shout back to Vadim. "Call and have the hotel switch the room over to me. I can pay for it. Have a good fucking night, Vadim. I hope you run into a beautiful escort, one-hundred percent your type who fleeces you for all you're worth."

"You really think you can walk back to the city?" he wonders in a voice like steel.

I flick my hair over my shoulder and walk faster. "Watch me."

He makes a sound between a grunt and scoff. Not even a full minute later, his sports car is racing past me, leaving me in the dust.

I wave at him with none of the decorum befitting a well-bred lady.

Then I suck in air, wobble on my heels, and the tears start coming down hard. I must get lost—enough for someone from the house to take pity on me. It isn't long before another car pulls up alongside me. The driver is the same kind-eyed figure who let me borrow his jacket.

"Can I give you a ride, Miss?" he says, his tone polite.

I sniffle and nod, climbing into the backseat.

Then I endure the ride into the city, plotting the next phase of my adventure—shameless, sexual revenge.

CHAPTER SEVEN

I can't actually afford the hotel room by myself. Realistically, anyway. I can last about three days tops, and that's if I completely decimate what little savings I have. I could always call my parents, but I've suffered enough of their pity to last a lifetime. Besides, I'd rather not deal with Daddy bribing me to come back home or hear my mother cry about "the state of my only little girl's life" one more time.

So I approach the front desk, ready and willing to swallow the cost no matter the pain.

"I'm sorry," the hostess informs me, frowning at her computer screen. "It looks like the room has already been paid in full for the week, complete with an open tab for room service."

I frown. Could Vadim be planning to claim the suite for himself? What a dick. He might already be there right now, screwing some blond escort submissive enough to fit his preferences.

"You are listed as the room's primary occupant," the hostess adds, scouring her records. "Ms. Connors, correct? It looks like the change was just freshly made. About an hour ago. I could always refund the card on record—"

"No." I turn on my heel and head for the elevator, squashing all doubt. "Thanks for your help."

I reenter the suite to find my bags where I left them and everything else in place, though neatly arranged, the bed turned down by some over-eager housekeeper.

So this must be Vadim's idea of the ultimate kiss-off. Leave me in an unfamiliar city. Pay off the incredibly expensive room he stuck me in. Leave without a trace.

And I thought Jim could be an asshole.

Dejected, I sink onto the bed and sob in earnest. I let out every ugly, choking, nasty cry and allow the tears to stream down my cheeks in earnest. Then I find the remote to a flat-screen TV hidden behind a pair of black curtains hanging across from the bed, turn to the music channels, and find the most upbeat pop imaginable. I play it as loud as I dare, shed my dress, and then hop into the bathroom and face myself in the mirror.

Years wasted in a loveless marriage can teach a girl a lot of things. Like that, no one—no gosh darn one—is worth losing your self-respect for. No one can make you feel any lower than you allow them to, and no one should ever rob you of your smile.

I smile now, displaying my teeth at the exhausted woman before me.

"You are confident," I tell her. "You are bold, and vivacious, and sexy. And—" A new addition to my mantra, but ad-libbing is all part of the exploration of freedom. "You are going to march into that sex club and own the darn place! Vadim, who?"

I manage to work the shower properly and then crawl into bed, feeling fresh and renewed. This might be a setback, sure.

Or it could be the real start to my adventures in sexual freedom.

I WAKE up and order from room service, half-convinced that the card on file will be declined, and Vadim Gorgoshev will have the last fucking laugh. But not even ten minutes later, my meal arrives steaming hot and I feel bold enough to write a generous tip on the napkin afterward with a message to charge to the account.

After changing into the blue dress from my shopping spree, I head down to the concierge and request assistance in finding a flight straight back to California, ASAP. Sure, I told Vadim I'd go to his little sex club and orgy myself silly. But that was just a boast made in the heat of the moment, right?

"I've found two flights, Miss," the concierge says, drawing my attention. "Both don't leave until tomorrow morning. Should I book one for you?"

"There isn't one sooner? Tonight, at least?"

He shakes his head apologetically. "I'm afraid not. Though, if you're looking to kill time, I've been informed that you are still authorized to use the town car should you require it."

"Alright, I'll take the earliest flight. Thanks anyway." Frowning, I accept the booking information he gives me and then return to the room, feeling more trapped than free.

But then I spot it. It being a platinum, no-limit, fancy smanshy credit card that Vadim gave me for my dress. I could have sworn

I'd returned it to him. Even thinking about using it now would be both illegal and reckless. Not to mention petty as hell.

Minutes later, I'm in the town car, directing William to the shopping district I'd scoped out yesterday. I find my favorite designer—whose clothing I couldn't afford guilt-free, even while on my parent's tap—and I march in, guns blazing.

I buy the sexiest dress I've ever seen in my entire life and shoes to match. And the purse. And the complementary faux fur stole and diamond-studded belt.

It's the outfit heist of the century, and I'm fully resigned to have the card declined as the salesgirl goes to ring me up. It's the thought that counts—one last screw you to the bastard who hurt me way more than I'd like to admit. Not just the whole *"I used you to embarrass my brother and his family because I am a dick"* thing. Maybe my irritation has less to do with that and more to do with…

The whole *"I don't want to fuck you, or get sucked off by you, and by the way, you're not even my type"* thing.

Hurt pride is a vengeful, nasty animal—one best soothed with lots of retail therapy.

"I'm sorry," I blurt as the saleswoman returns, brandishing the card. "My husband probably cut me off. It's for the best—"

"Having cold feet?" she wonders, glancing at my spoils of war. "It went through, but if you like, I can cancel the charges?"

"No!" I lurch to my feet, my thirst for vengeance suddenly renewed. "I'll take them all, please. And let's throw in one or two of those brooches to match. And I'd love to see your jewelry collection. And how about some more shoes?"

WILLIAM DRIVES me to the address listed on Vadim's little sex club calling card, and my cheeks burn the entire trip. My heart skips too, partly terrified, partly excited.

I don't know what to expect when the car finally comes to a stop before this mysterious Club XXX.

A place that looks like the gate to a sleek, exclusive corner of hell, isn't it. My mouth falls open as I take in the remote building formed of bold, eye-catching lines. It's a gothic mixture of the macabre and the modern. Turrets stab at the indigo sky, creating a striking silhouette against a forested backdrop. The entrance itself consists of stone columns framing a black door, trimmed in glittering gold. A stone path leads to it before forking into a massive circular driveway like some beckoning gesture.

Any doubt I felt dissolves as my lips part into a massive grin. Color me impressed.

I approach the door warily, discovering no doorman or bouncer waiting to deny entry. It's as if the act of palming the handle itself is the only method required—a dare all on its own. *Are you even brave enough?*

I hold my breath as I push my way inside, entering a world of black marble and gray walls ripped right from my most deranged fantasies. Granite floors accent the circular foyer, making every footstep echo times a thousand. There is no sign, it seems, proclaiming "sex rooms this way." Just three silver Xs adorning the space above a curving archway across from the entrance serving as the only advertisement. Two other arches frame it, each leading off into different directions.

Pulsating music emanating from the leftmost one serves to cast a mysterious aura, and all I can do is see where it takes me.

I follow a wide hall to another archway and discover my first clue that the place isn't entirely deserted. A man stands beside it, dressed in a black shirt and slacks. Authority radiates from his stern gaze and, without thinking, I hand him the business card.

"Vadim sent me?" Why I make it a question, I have no idea.

He looks it over and then nods, presumably giving me permission to enter.

Here goes nothing…

I take a few steps forward and nearly faint. What at first looks like a typical—though decadent—lounge turns out to be so much more on second glance. A long ebony-topped bar dominates one end, and an L-shaped stage divides the room in half on the other. Crowning the space is a row of floor-to-ceiling windows providing a view of the darkness beyond.

And it is better than I could have hoped.

Décor consisting of black leather with bright drops of blood-red accents crafts such a sexy allure I almost squeal. The icing on the cake, however, is the clientele milling about the massive room. Everyone here makes my red party dress from last night look like a nun's frock in comparison. Beautiful women wear strips of leather and silk masquerading as dresses while men shamelessly parade in a mixture of suits or less.

I instantly feel oddly…at home. When an elegantly clad server comes to take my jacket, I relinquish it eagerly. And with renewed determination, I delve into my newly found freedom.

CHAPTER EIGHT

I know firsthand that the absolute worst thing you can do to someone is pretend that they no longer exist. Not in the petty, childish way you might ostracize them on the playground. No. This level of indifference requires skill and tact. You acknowledge the person, of course. You simper and utter all the right niceties as if they were anyone else—that's the key to it. As if they were anyone else. Someone meaningless without a string of memories attached to them.

Someone whose name didn't require remembering.

Someone worthless. Thus, such is the ultimate blow I swore I would never ever inflict upon someone no matter how much I hated them.

Until now. Hate has nothing to do with it, just pride. So the icy cool businessman came to see how I would play in his world? Well, I can thrive, regardless of his presence.

Let him watch and learn.

He arrives just when I start to let my guard down enough to take a stool at the bar. Acclimating to a debauched club is a surprisingly gradual experience. One can't merely jump in and star in a six-person gang bang right out of the gate. Fitting in requires confidence and finesse—like the time when I felt old enough to enter the sauna at my parent's country club. I couldn't let my unease show on my face or Barb—a bitchy socialite who liked to gossip in said sauna—would have sent me out on my butt the second I entered.

No. I had to play the game and meld seamlessly into the background. Which I've been doing here, until now. It's not like I'm waiting for him to show up—but the entire room notices when he does.

Dressed in a black suit tailored close to his frame, the bastard arrives with an aura comparable to a king making an entrance with a full retinue. Though alone, he oozes…ownership. Like he's too good to step foot in this club, let alone fuck anyone in it. He's merely here to observe, for his own entertainment.

And it seems I may be his main attraction. Is his aim to gloat? His eyes dart in my direction, and I turn away, keeping my smile intact. Inside, I'm seething, and when the bartender appears before me, I order my Achilles heel.

"A sangria, please," I say. "Don't water it down."

He nods, and then I scan my nearest surroundings for someone, anyone. I told him I was going to spend my night sucking cock. Well, darn it, that's just what I'll do. On my third perusal of the room, I notice a man advancing in my direction. Dressed in a tailored suit, he's probably a businessman and disgustingly rich.

When he raises a sensually questioning eyebrow, I simper in response. *Target acquired.* I beckon him over with a wave just as my Sangria arrives to provide my reckless impulses extra ammunition.

He's tall. Blond. Not my type, but why does it matter? His body isn't bad to look at, and when he smiles, he's easy on the eyes if a bit older than I would have aimed for.

"I'm Tiffy," I tell him, extending my hand.

"Geoff," he replies in a husky baritone. "Pleased to make your acquaintance—" He breaks off suddenly and smoothly withdraws his hand. "I'm sorry. I didn't realize you were here with someone."

"Huh?" Following his alarmed gaze, I look over my shoulder and stiffen. Perched on a black couch nearly halfway across the room, Vadim sits facing my direction, a whiskey glass in hand. Judging from his casual, relaxed position, I don't think he's moved or said anything to give the impression we were together—but the expression on his face…

I feel a tug in my belly as if an invisible hook has caught the flesh and yanked. It's certainly not how he looked at me in the Six lounge, that's for darn sure. Mocking. Daring. …Possessive?

Easy, Tiffy, my inner bitch warns. *Eye on the prize.*

I blink innocently and squint at the aloof billionaire. Then I sigh and shake my head. "I'm sorry, but you're mistaken," I tell Geoff, turning back to him. "I've never seen that man before in my life."

"Oh." He frowns, confused, only to blink in shock when I palm his bicep, testing the give of the muscle. He's no surprisingly-built, slender waif, but he feels solid enough. Satisfied, I shift toward him and let my eyes glaze over, my smile warm.

"I'm here all alone," I tell him. "Keep me company?"

He grabs a nearby stool and pulls up beside me while I sip frantically on my sangria. By the time he brushes my hand, drawing my attention, my confident grin is back in place.

"Come here often?" he wonders, while internally, I cringe at what had been my tired and worn pick-up line not too long ago. Had it sounded so darn cliché when I said it?

No wonder Vadim lost interest.

Still smiling, I shake my head and eye him through my lashes. "This is my first time," I say, utilizing my sexy purr once more.

He falls for the bait hook, line, and sinker. His hand grazes my thigh as he grips the edge of my stool and tugs me closer to his.

"I could tell," he says confidently. "You look fresh. There is nothing like your first time, eh? I'm curious as to how a girl like you even found your way in a place like this."

Gag. Maintaining my simpering grin suddenly takes more effort, my teeth clenched. "I know a guy," I say.

Geoff raises an eyebrow, impressed. "You must have friends in high places. I feel like I had to sell my soul just to get an invite. The owner is selective as hell."

I file away the information for later. For some reason, I suspect he isn't referring to Vadim, given he didn't seem to recognize him. Who could his business partner be, I wonder?

"There are several owners actually," Geoff adds. "But Maxim runs this part of the club. If you're here, I assume you've heard of its reputation?" He glances me over, lingering on my cleavage while I take another sip of wine to disguise my shock.

Maxim owns this? His brother. I risk sneaking a glance at Vadim, more confused than ever. Zap! Our eyes meet with a jolt—it's like he knew I'd look at him. Knew I'd jump and turn away just in time to catch him sipping from his glass.

Damn it.

"Are you alright?" Geoff tucks a piece of my hair behind my ear, his tone concerned.

I nod, fighting to stay focused. "I'm fine." To prove it, I fixate stubbornly on his mouth, refusing to look anywhere else. Even as the back of my neck prickles with the uncomfortable knowledge that someone is watching *me*, daring me to notice.

"I'm looking for a teacher," I murmur, inclining my head to display my throat. "I'm very, *very* eager to learn."

"Good," Geoff murmurs, his smile dashing.

This is good. Better than good. Barely ten minutes in, and I've successfully infiltrated my first sex club. I even scored my first test subject. All is well.

As far as my list is concerned, *check, check.*

So why the hell am I shaking?

"I could oblige you," Geoff says with a resonating laugh. "I take it you don't have a private room yet?"

I sit forward, curious enough to ignore everything else. Private, he says? Whatever it is sounds absolutely delicious. I decide on the spot that I must experience one before the night's end. "No," I say. "For now."

"Good." He grabs a napkin and fishes a pen from his breast pocket. After scribbling a number onto the corner of it, he hands the napkin to me. "Come join me when you've finished your drink. I'll head up first and…prepare it for your first lesson." He looks me over from head to toe, and any other day I would be elated by the attention. Actual, lustful male attention.

As it stands, all I feel is…anxious. My palms are slick, my heart racing. I must still be hungover.

"Let me walk you out," I suggest as Geoff starts for the exit. I step up to him, linking my arm with his. "So, I can see which direction you go."

We start for the main hall and nearly run smack dab into a man who seemingly appears from nowhere to rudely block our path.

"Pardon," Geoff hisses.

I merely smile sweetly and pat the stranger on his arm as I would do for anyone who nearly ran me over. "Excuse me," I say, slipping past him.

Deep down, I sense something in the atmosphere shift—a warning drop in the air pressure like the kind that proceeds a bad storm. Oblivious, Geoff runs his fingers down my arm and then enters the hall, heading for an archway opposite the club floor.

"There are the stairs," he tells me. "The rooms are on the second floor."

"Ah," I nod and flutter my eyelashes. The second he's gone from view, I retreat to the bar and down my sangria as if it's the antidote to nerves. I'm not approached once. When I finally finish, I enter the hall while telling myself with every step that I can do this.

I had sex with one stranger on a drunken whim. What's another? And hopefully another?

But this pang in my chest won't ease no matter how many ways I envision sucking off Geoff. The stairs he referenced lurk at the end of another hall and curve to join a split-level landing that overlooks the main foyer, unseen from the first floor. The rooms themselves must be behind a row of polished, ebony doors. Geoff's is apparently near the end.

Sighing, I square my shoulders and march forward. *You can do this, Tiffy. One step after the other…*

Or not. A hand grabs my arm, and someone drags me into a room at least four doors away from Geoff. Stunned, I wrench away from them and whirl around, a scream poised at the back of my throat.

In the end, it escapes my lips as a hiss instead.

Vadim glowers, looking so beautiful it hurts. His eyes are even more electric, his jaw clenched, his posture broadcasting authority. It's such a contrast to his icy, closed-off persona from the other night. I feel my throat dampen.

At least before I remember that I hate him.

"What do you want?" I demand when he doesn't speak. "To have me mentally scar a few more children?" I gesture to my outfit— it's ten times more revealing than my ensemble from last night. A black, skintight mini dress leaves little to the imagination, and two slits on either side go up so high they might as well touch my armpits.

"You came." Vadim's eyes rake over me, dark and unreadable. I came—and he doesn't sound too thrilled about that. Why? Did he really think I'd run back to Cali and let him keep his little club all to himself?

"Leave me alone," I snap, ignoring how his gaze lingers over my partially exposed breasts. Turning on my heel, I march for the door.

"Wait—" He grasps my wrist, yanking me right back.

"What?" I whip around to face him again, snatching my hand back. "Why are you even here?"

"Curiosity," he grates coldly, though I get the sense that he responded to me without thinking. His attention is otherwise consumed—rapt, his gaze traces me again, and I can't suppress a shiver in response. "I wondered if you were serious," he murmurs, eyeing an exposed sliver of my hip. "Or…"

"Ha!" I throw my head back for a nasty laugh. "Or if I was bluffing? Oh, I was *so* serious. Bachelor number one is already lined up. Curious as to how you stack up? Stick around, and you just may find out."

"I…apologize," he grits out, as if it physically pains him to admit as much. "If you were offended."

"Offended?" I don't know whether to laugh at him or give him the finger. "You treated me like a stupid slut. Of course, I was offended. Now get out of my way!"

"*Ta gueule*," he hisses, shifting to block my path once more. "Let me speak—"

"Don't you dare cuss at me in another language," I snarl, recognizing his tone though I don't understand the term. French? "And listen to you? I think not. Now, excuse me, stranger whom I've never met before. Stop following me." I wave him off with a haughty flick of my fingers. "If you don't mind, I'm about to get laid—"

"Wait!" He snatches my forearm the second I take a step toward the door. This time I lash out, gasping as my hand bounces harmlessly against his chest. He steps into me, grasping my chin.

Before I can react, his lips capture mine, silencing me with a brutal kiss that leaves my mind reeling.

It's…hot. Really hot. He grips my hips, his fingers fanning out. Then he breaks off and shoves me toward a leather chaise. I lean over it, scrambling to find my balance.

But he's already behind me. His fingers plunge beneath my skirt, and a vicious sound rips from his throat.

Again, I've forsaken any panties, a fact that he takes advantage of with a swift, deliberate thrust of what feels like his thumb.

Holy crap. My startled moan rings out. This isn't like how he touched me before. Gone is the mocking, persistent wall. His finger trembles with barely concealed restraint. Like it's taking everything he has in him not to rake with his nails. Shove inside me. Grip. Mark. Hurt.

The worst part? Something sick inside of me kind of wants him to.

"Are you going to just tease me again?" I wonder mockingly. "Fuck me half-assed and then kick me to the curb?"

He goes rigid, and I chuckle in triumph, scooting away from him.

"I thought so. Now, if you'll excuse me, I have a *real* fuck waiting to be experienced—"

He grabs me hard, shoving me face down against the leather. Panic prickles through my nerves, but a stronger emotion keeps the fear at bay for now. Excitement.

The hands wrenching up the skirt of my dress aren't polished and mocking anymore. They ruthlessly feel along my skin, palming my ass. I hiss in irritation when they withdraw only to…

Thwack! My eyelids flutter as fire sears through my left cheek—the kind of pain caused by only one act.

"D-Did you just spank me?" I question through clenched teeth, horrified. As if in apology, his palm cups me again, smoothing over the stinging flesh. He withdraws…only to assault the same spot again. Harder—*definitely* a spanking.

My mouth waters at the realization, my knees buckling. Throat rasping, all I can think to say is, "Do it again…"

He doesn't. Instead, he must grab a chunk of my hair, using it to yank my head back. I whimper as the pain sears through my scalp. It actually hurts.

It hurts so good.

Sweat mists my skin as I arch my hips, seeking out more contact. Touching. Anything. Disappointed when he doesn't deliver a single caress, I scoff, my laughter harsh.

"Are you going to fuck me with your wall up?" I taunt him, rolling my eyes up to the ceiling—the only thing I have a clear view of from this position. "Sorry, Vadim. Been there. Done that. Got the postcard and it wasn't all it was cracked up to—"

"*Merde.*" The foreign word rips from him as he tests me with his thumb, finding me dripping. "You enjoy this?" he mutters, his voice rasping with confusion.

Enjoy? My brain takes that word and runs with it, translating it from brooding billionaire speak to English—*won. Trapped. Conquered.*

I made him come here, to a venue he seems to hate, run by a brother he loathes. I've reduced him to this—a creature ruled by lust, too far gone to hold back. He'll take what he wants.

I whimper at the telltale hum of a zipper being undone. The hiss of shifting fabric. Then I feel him pulsating against me, and my brain threatens to turn off for good.

"I thought I'm not your type," I tell him spitefully, even though he feels so good I almost hate myself for trying to deter him. He's a delicious conduit of heat, prodding my lower lips, feeling thicker than before. Intimidating. One experimental buck of his hips forces him a fraction inside me, drawing a groan from my mouth. But when he thrusts for real, I can't silence a scream.

He goes deep, lacking his previous restraint. His next thrust is even harder. Ruthless.

It's everything I never knew I wanted, and my brain can't cope. I go blank, drugged on the sensation as he manipulates me like a rag doll, driving in so fiercely my teeth chatter with the violent motions. Somewhere at the back of my mind, I know he's snarling in frustration, spitting out a mixture of English and that other mysterious language.

While my mewling, throaty cries easily overpower him.

"Is this—" His hips slam into me, rocking my body against the back of the couch. I have to scramble like I'm trying to crawl over it, just to find enough stability to push back, ridding every stroke he has to give. "What—" Another thrust. "You wanted?"

A *punishing* thrust nearly robs me of my voice. Gasping, I answer him mindlessly. "Yes, yes, yes. So good. More, more."

I stimulate my inner muscles to grip him hard, testing his resolve. If anything, the challenge seems to spur him into snatching my hips, yanking me into him. Groaning, he works to shove past each rippling, grasping contraction. His cock swells, sowing friction that has my toes curling in my heels.

I think my brain explodes.

The next thing I know, an orgasm is tearing through me so strongly I can only grit my teeth and ride it out, wave after brutal wave. Even in my daze, I sense the moment he seems to pull back. Come to his senses. Try to reassemble his wall before it's too late.

"No!" I wiggle my hips shamelessly, humping him like some porno star. "Come in me, please, please, please."

He swipes his hand over my lower back—hesitating? Then he grips me hard, his nails sinking in. All I can do is seize the edge of the couch and hold on as he bucks into me, grunting. Groaning.

Then he shudders, and it's like I can track the tension building within him, riding up his cock and finally exploding from him in reckless, ruthless waves.

And it's the most amazing thing I've ever felt. Tears spill down my cheeks, my grin wild, my laughter shrill with triumph.

But then, somewhere within the come down, I realize…

I just fucked a human switchblade.

CHAPTER NINE

I don't know how we got here. *Here* being my hotel room, I think. I barely remember leaving the club. Entering a fancy red sports car. Having someone practically drag me into an elevator. Then, stripping my clothes and frantically trying to undress someone else—who stubbornly refused to remove more than his suit jacket and undo some of his shirt buttons. We stumbled into the bedroom afterward, and…

Hmm. Everything's starting to blur and run together—but who cares?

I now have two glasses of wine, one in each hand. A beautiful man lies beneath me while I straddle him on a massive, luxurious bed. It's heaven on earth, even if a part of me whispers that it's a lie.

"You're mean," I tell Vadim seriously. So sexy and so mean. "What you did was really mean. I shouldn't even be talking to you!" I lift my arms in indignation and wind up sloshing wine over the sliver of his chest bared by his partially undone shirt.

Oops. Before a single drop can stain the tailored cotton garment, I lower my mouth to his pec and lick him clean. All better.

"Mean," he echoes, sounding amused once more. He stares up at me, his gaze crystal clear. I doubt he's taken a single sip of the wine he procured for me. No matter. That just means there's more for me.

"Yes!" I nod. Then I giggle. "Spanking me was very mean, but in that case, you have my permission."

"I should do more than spank you." He's frowning, his gaze distant. "My brother rarely speaks to me," he adds, gripping my hips to steady me while I continue to bounce in place. "Never has he reached out genuinely. Not once. This morning, he sent you a present—well, I'm sure his fiancée had a hand in it, but your name is on the box."

"Presents?" I perk up and scan the room. "Where?"

He nods to indicate a glass table positioned near the windows.

With a giddy squeal, I shimmy to the edge of the mattress and allow him to assist me by taking my wine glasses. Staggering on jellied legs, I find a beautifully wrapped package complete with a small handwritten note.

Thank you for the thoughtful gifts, someone had written. *Francesca and Maxim.*

I marvel at the simple gesture. Maxim may be scary as hell, but maybe there is some hope for him yet? At the moment, I'm tipsy enough to give even the Devil himself the benefit of the doubt.

"How sweet!" Feeling like a kid on Christmas morning, I rip into the package and gape at the present within. "Oh! It's so pretty." And luxurious too—a beautiful ruby-colored shawl made of silk.

I drape it around my shoulders and find something else tucked within the box. "They sent you something as well." I lift the navy colored piece of fabric and unfurl it, revealing a very nice tie. Lurching to my feet, I spin around only to find Vadim behind me. He eyes the strip of fabric as though it's poisonous.

"So skeptical you are." Giggling, I loop the tie around his neck only to instantly regret the finished effect. "Blue is so your color," I tell him, annoyed at that fact. Navy enhances the depth of his gaze, making his eyes seem even more intense than usual. No fair.

"Do you make a habit out of manipulating people into giving you what you want?" he wonders grudgingly.

I bristle at that. "Not uh! It's the first rule of engagement." I lift my finger, about to school him on the proper gifting protocol, otherwise known as social norms. "Never arrive to a party without a gift for the hosts. Always shower them with adequate compliments. And…" I trail off, frowning as my thoughts turn fuzzy. "Something about always asking for seconds, even if the food tastes like ass, I think. Can I have my wines back, please?"

He frowns, so surly. "I'm starting to wonder if I should cut you off…"

I gasp in mock horror and snatch one glass right from his hand. "Never! I'm free, and no one can tell me what to do, remember? Not even you. It's on my list."

To prove it, I skip over to the window and admire the view of the city outstretched below, like a smattering of diamonds. If I stand at the right angle, I can make out my reflection—tall, butt-naked, swaying in the shadow of a larger, more enigmatic figure.

"Come here." I beckon Vadim until he reluctantly steps forward, and then I sigh. "We look so sexy together." And we do. Fire and embers. Light and dark. "What a shame that you're so mean."

"Why shouldn't I be?" he counters. His hand smooths over my hip, and I arch into the contact. Then he stiffens as if he realizes only now what he's done. Touch me of his own free will.

"Mean?" I prod before guzzling from my wine. I resurface pleasantly buzzed and add, "Because it's mean!"

"In my world, you learn quickly that it's better to be on your guard," he muses. His words nuzzle the nape of my neck, and he's even closer. "People seek out others only to gain something they want. I'm just prudent enough to ensure that more often than not, I get my desired win first. Consider that *my* version of a list. The first rule is to always anticipate the selfishness of others. The second someone believes they have what you seek, they own you."

It sounds so cutthroat. So darkly sexy.

"I didn't want anything from you," I point out, draining my glass. "I mean, I did, but mainly I wanted to do things *to* you. Sexy things. You wouldn't let me."

A low hum resonates through his chest, and I nearly drop my empty glass.

"Will you let me do them now, I wonder?" With a mischievous grin, I slink around, grinding my body into his, relishing the stern, impassive reaction. His obvious restraint makes the thrill so much better than what I figure Geoff's lust would inspire. Lust is boring. But Vadim? He's unpredictable, proven to snap once pushed to his breaking point.

So I *push*, bracing my hand on his chest to urge him back, back, back until he has to sit on the edge of the bed, staring up at me with a questioning gaze.

"I wanted so badly to suck you off," I announce, licking the rim of my glass for emphasis. From the corner of my eye, I watch him tense, his nostrils flaring, eyes narrowing. Holy crap. My inner thighs clench, and I fight to ignore the reaction. "I wanted to take you deep," I add, intrigued as his breaths quicken in response. "So deep. I wanted to practice all the new skills I've read about. It wouldn't have been perfect, but I'm sure it would have been good." I'm still violating my wine glass shamelessly. I lick all the way around the rim and then swirl my tongue through the opening while holding his gaze. "Your size is impressive, but I'm sure I could have deepthroated you."

He sits forward, flattening his hands over his knees, his legs parted ominously. "Kneel."

A thrill of excitement runs through me so quickly I almost fan myself. Instead, I turn my back to him as I consider complying or crawling into bed and waiting for my hangover to kick in. All it takes is one look at him in the reflection on the window for me to bend—slowly—and set my glass on the floor.

When I stand and face him again, he's still wearing the same hard, unreadable expression. But as I sidle over to him, a muscle in his jaw quirks.

"Kneel?" I parrot him innocently. "Like this?" Stopping short just beyond his reach, I sink gracefully to my knees, my head bowed. When I gather the nerve to peek at him, he's unmoving, his eyes flashing. He's too proud to even command me.

But there's a distinct bulge tenting the front of his slacks, too tempting to resist, my pride be damned. I crawl to him, licking my lips in anticipation. When I finally come close enough to reach for the fastenings of his pants, he doesn't shy away.

Trembling with the anticipation, I unwrap him with far more care than I did my present. I peel the fabric back slowly, all while squeezing slightly to test the hardness lurking beneath.

He grunts, sounding pained. His clenched teeth betray that he's trying his damned hardest to suppress any noise at all. I'm not so composed.

"Gosh," I murmur, once his cock is freed. "So, so pretty. So beautiful." I kiss the smooth, bulbous end for emphasis—and I think Mr. Vadim nearly comes out of his skin.

That's all I do at first—feather kisses up and down his length, the more of him I coax free. I even tease the ends of his piercing. He has his own unique taste that I find myself craving, tainted with remnants of me. Should be gross in theory, I suspect. In reality…

"We even taste good together," I murmur to him, in case he was wondering. What a shame he can be such a dick. Mournfully, I flick my tongue along the underside of him, testing the give of the largest, pulsating vein surging beneath. I think I could come from this alone—exploring him lazily, drunk off both sex and wine.

But now it's time for the finale. I honestly don't know where to start—the women in pornos make it look so easy. Letting impulse guide me, I part my lips around the crown and swirl my tongue. But then it's like the second my mouth closes over his shaft, instinct kicks in.

An electric impulse jolts down my spine, guiding my movements. Slow at first. Then harder, using my hand to pump his length where my mouth can't reach. He hardens darn near instantly, thickening to make even taking his tip a struggle.

But I'm eager to keep going. Try harder. Please him as much as humanly possible. Because when he moans…

A choir of singing angels couldn't compare to the sound. Nothing else in the world could ever come close to this man, grunting in pleasure, fisting his hands through my hair like he's losing his mind just as rapidly as I am.

"*Merde*," he swears throatily. "*Je n'ai jamais…* Fuck."

Spurred on by the reaction, I lunge into him, taking him further. More. Deepthroating him isn't an option, but maybe one day. I could learn to let him in, down my throat—and the mere idea of it sets me off like a match striking gasoline.

My fingers jab between my legs, seeking out my clit as I suck, caressing him with my tongue, urging him in wordless moans.

And then it happens. He goes rigid, his fingers practically tearing out my hair. His cock jerks against my lips, and then I feel it. Taste it.

His release, coming so quickly, he couldn't hold back even if he tried.

Holy, freaking crap.

My eyes roll into the back of my head as I work to swallow. But it's too much. *He* is too much. Excess dribbles down my chin, speckling my tits, and I've never felt filthier. And it feels so, darn, good to be filthy with him. Better than good.

And I could cry with the conflicting emotions washing through me as I back away from him, gasping for air. "See how good it can be when you give me what I want?" I tell him accusingly. "I give you what you need…"

Something he might contest, I realize once I meet his gaze. Rather than dazed with ecstasy, he looks so…angry. Furious, even. Color paints his elegant cheeks, tightening the corner of his mouth and enhancing the darkness of his irises.

Abruptly, he stands, letting his pants fall down to the floor. One by one, he kicks his legs to shed the garment completely, then he advances and palms my skull, sinking his fingers through my hair. A gentle tug warns me to rise along with him, craning my neck back. He forces my head near his, his breath fanning my lips. Tension builds the longer his dark eyes scour mine.

The good thing to do would be wait and see. But I can't. His nearness feels so darn tempting. I'm the kid in the candy store all over again. Straining his grip, I stand on tiptoe and brush my lips over his. Again. He frowns, resisting me as I nudge his more firmly, urging them apart. Thinking quickly, I flick my tongue along his lower lip. Success. He opens his mouth, nipping me in return, and…

It's sin.

Kissing him is a new realm, so different from the sex. He can shield himself from me, even while railing my brains out. But like this? I'm poking through a crack in his wall when we're like this. Eager to explore, I palm both sides of his head and wiggle my hips into him. His hair feels like silk, his body perfection. My brain swims, overheating, oozing out of my mouth as mindless nonsense.

"You feel so good," I murmur against his parted lips. How can *anyone* feel so good?

But it's as if my excitement flips a switch in him. *Bam!* His wall goes up in record time, forcing me to withdraw completely or risk having my tongue sliced in half by the falling action. His jaw hardens against me, his head cocking, that cold expression returning.

"You hate when I praise you," I point out, waggling my finger at him in disapproval. *Bingo.* His gaze darkens, withdrawn, and mistrustful. Sighing, I flounce away from him and dive onto the bed.

"Sorry to break it to you, Vadim—" I roll over to face him and deliberately suck in a lungful of air. His brows furrow as if he's reading my mind, and he starts forward, mounting the mattress in my wake. "You fuck REALLY GOOD!" I scream it at the top of my lungs, cackling as he grips my chin to silence me. I look up at him, enthralled by the planes of his face and those gorgeous freaking eyes. And his mouth, still wet from our kiss. I wonder if he's one of those guys who hates tasting the results of sex. That could explain the hot and cold action to an extent. But no. Even as I watch, his tongue traces a dangerous path from one end of his mouth to the other.

And my toes curl helplessly.

"You should put your mouth on me," I tell him, pleading. "Just once. To make up for hurting me. I'd love you then, forever and ever."

"It only takes oral sex to buy your love?" he wonders mockingly.

"My love? No!" I push on his chest, thrilled when he lets me manipulate him onto his back and straddle him. Between my legs seems to be the one position where I feel like I have the advantage. He's easier to read from this angle. "My love would cost a lot more than that. Like, the entire new Chanel spring collection in every color levels of dedication. But for now, to buy my *maybe* forgiveness, I'll settle for you telling me why. Why did you go through all of that trouble for something so spiteful? It would have been way easier to just pick up a real hooker on your way there."

"Why?" He shrugs and palms my hips with both hands, keeping me in place. "My brother brings out the worst in me," he says.

As if that explains it. Though maybe it does. I know firsthand what it's like to have someone bring out the parts of you better left buried. Jim is my case and point.

"What happened between the two of you?"

"It's a story that isn't worth retelling," he says with one of those devious, secretive smiles.

"What about the other man? Milton?" I ask. "Who is he?"

His smile wavers. "A friend. More of a brother to me than Maxim in so many ways. Some could say we grew up together…"

He sounds so wistful. Honest. I marvel at the rare hint of vulnerability, and like a vulture, I can't resist nibbling.

"Tell me more?"

His expression glazes over, and like magic, the wall comes back up. "There isn't more."

I frown and poke him in the center of his chest. "Where are my wines?" I wonder, glancing around the room.

"You drank one," he reminds me. "I left the other…over here." He shifts beneath me and reaches for a nearby end table, withdrawing my glass from the edge of it.

"Thank you very much," I simper, holding out my hand for it.

"Should I do the responsible thing and pour it out, I wonder?"

I gasp in mock horror and lean down to steal a sip right from the rim. "It would be a sin to waste such a perfect vintage. But maybe I should slow down just a tad…"

He obediently sets the glass aside while I roll off of him and stare up at the ceiling. For whatever reason, he remains beside me.

"You know, if you kept me around, I could smooth things over between you and your brother in no time flat." I snap my fingers for emphasis.

"I would hate to dampen your enthusiasm," he remarks, "but I doubt even your skills could help much in this instance."

He sounds so sure of that. Disappointed, even?

"Never doubt the skills of a basic bitch from California," I tell him solemnly. "It's a damn good thing we aren't compatible. A mere week with me, and you'd wake up to find your bachelor pad now a pastel hell designed by Laura Ashley, and that you and your brother have a weekly golf game every Sunday."

"A tempting future," he murmurs. The weird part? I can't tell if he's being serious or not.

Rolling onto my side, I tap his jaw with the tip of my finger. "But you'll never have it," I tell him.

"Is that so?" His voice drips down to that amused, delicious murmur and something inside me quivers. Fearful? Excited? I can't tell.

"You'll have to buy my forgiveness first, and I don't see any Chanel bags. Besides." I scoot away from him and shimmy beneath the covers. "You'll pull your mysterious billionaire act and disappear before the morning, which is just fine with me because I have a plane to catch. Try not to let the door hit ya on the way out," I add with a forced yawn. "I'm a light sleeper."

"And if I decide to stay in the room that *my* accounts are paying for?" he wonders tonelessly.

"You won't." True regret slips into my voice before I can help it. "That would require letting down your wall, dear Sir. Something you seem to have trouble doing around me."

Even now, he's playing along, saying the right things. But something tells me that's all he's doing—playing. The real Vadim hides behind an ironclad façade, and I only see glimpses when I taunt him enough into coming out.

Sure enough, I sense the mattress lighten, suddenly devoid of his weight.

"It would be a shame to waste this room since it's already been paid in full for the entire week," he muses.

I burrow deeper beneath the blankets and pout in secret. "Maybe you'll find some escort to play with while I'm gone?"

"I may."

I peek from beneath the blankets and watch him leave every bit as inconspicuously as he had arrived at the club. Dominating the entire room.

And then stealing the air with him, making the world feel chilled and suffocating in his absence.

CHAPTER TEN

I wake up too hungover to function. All I can do is moan in agony and stumble into the shower. Ritual healing performed, I can start to piece together the events of the previous night, all while trying not to die in utter mortified shame.

I had sex with Vadim again. Technically twice. Once in an alarmingly rough display, I'd pour over later, and then again when I finally got to fellate him for real.

And what an experience that was. I feel like a child who discovered that Santa, magic, and the Tooth fairy are all real—but surprise! You can only see them on a particular full moon, at midnight, only if you stand on one foot and squint in the right spot, and it's already the morning after. The opportunity has sadly passed, never to return again.

Unfair.

The smart thing to do would be to get on the first plane back to California and put this whirlwind excursion behind me. Luckily, I have a flight leaving in…soon, I think. Frowning, I shimmy into a towel and run through the room, searching for the itinerary documents I had the concierge print out for me. I'm panting by the time I find them, and when I reconcile the time of my booked flight with the current time flashing on the LED alarm clock by the bed, I groan in despair.

"Damn it!"

A second later, the phone rings, and I lunge toward it, hoping beyond hope that it's an airline representative offering to hold the plane just in time for me to race across town and board.

"Hello?"

"Morning," a suave voice replies, and I bite down a groan. So sexy. So smug. My heart pangs as my belly clenches—two polar opposite reactions. "It seems you've decided to occupy the room another day after all."

"W-Wrong," I stammer while collapsing onto the end of the bed. "You've just caught me in the middle of packing. I'm on my way to the airport. My flight leaves soon."

"Wrong," he counters smoothly. "Your flight has been canceled. The next plane doesn't leave until tomorrow morning. All of this, you would know if you were already at the airport for your eight am flight, or if you were awake for any one of the ten wake-up calls, the hotel receptionist attempted to place to inform you. I'm alerted by email when you don't answer, you see. It appears that punctuality is not your forte, Ms. Connors."

I sigh in defeat. There's no arguing with that. "I can't help wondering if you got me drunk on purpose, Mr. Gorgoshev. If you wanted to keep me here so badly, you could have offered me the use of your private jet," I point out. "I would have gladly graced you with my presence for at least another day."

But now? I'd consider renting a car and driving cross country myself just to get out of his orbit.

"Where are you?" I ask him before he can reply. "Attending to more mysterious business meetings?"

"Something like that," he says. "I'm in the process of interviewing women."

My nose wrinkles. That's a weird way to phrase it. "For a secretarial position?"

"No. To be my wife."

I hang up automatically and back away from the phone as if burned. *Ouch. Ouch. Ouch.* I never knew rejection could sting so badly, and I've survived a messy divorce fit for tabloid fodder. Gosh, it's not even what he said that makes my stomach roil as if I'll vomit. It's how he said it. So mockingly. So matter of fact. *I'm interviewing women to be my wife*—which is a weird concept within itself—*but hahaha, Tiffany. You may have fucked me and sucked me, but you aren't even on my shortlist.*

Not that I would want to be, because what kind of person interviews marriage candidates? Someone so jaded and mistrustful he has an invisible wall built up wherever he goes.

And now I'm forced to spend another night in the same damn city as him.

Chin up, Tiffy, my inner bitch snarls. *Remember those promises you made to yourself? Put them to the test bitch! Start with your morning routine—let no one ever get you down.*

Right. Blinking back any tears, I find the music channel on the television and turn up the volume. Today's choice is vulgar, offensive feminine rap, and I loudly chant along to the lyrics while sifting through my past impulse purchases for something to wear. It is as I enthusiastically prattle along to the words, "Y'all men ain't shit," that I'm struck with a glorious revelation.

Fuck Vadim Gorgoshev—not literally but figuratively. He's left me in a gorgeous hotel suite, with room service already included, and I have not one but three designer gowns to choose from, membership to a sex club, and time to kill.

Geoff may have been a false start, but no worries. I'll find someone even better to fuck me senseless until my flight in the morning, Vadim and his new wife be damned.

Grinning, I settle on the black option he'd rejected as my party ensemble. Then I blow my hair out into loose waves and find the reddest lipstick from the handful I picked up the other day.

"You look gorgeous, Tiffy," I tell the bombshell beaming at me in the mirror's reflection. "Now go knock 'em dead."

I STROLL into the hotel bar as if I own the place. Screw private businessmen lounges or exclusive clubs. I'll take whoever I can get. It's being picky that got me into this mess in the first place.

With my shoulders back, head held high, I stroll into the sleek, modern setting feeling more confident than ever—and I almost run right back out.

This time of day, there are slim pickings as far as available men go—but one of the most eligible and hands down the most handsome of the prospects, sits at a table smack dab in the center of the room. I'll have to walk past him to reach the bar at the back, but that's not the worst part.

Seated across from him, as beautiful as if she stepped off of a runway, is a slender brunette with tousled curls, perfectly applied makeup, and a modest two-piece suit ensemble in a delicate shade of ivory. Paired with Vadim, they look like some sexy, uber-rich power couple, and my confidence plummets through the floor.

Damaged pride almost drives me away. Almost. But then I make my grin as wide as I can and approach Vadim's table casually. *Very* casually.

Thinking on the spot, I wave at him, brimming with enthusiasm as those dark eyes narrow in suspicion. Skipping to his side, I lean over him from behind and place my hand on his shoulder. He stiffens instantly, even more so as I bring my mouth near his ear and murmur loud enough for his table companion to hear me.

"Baby, when you're done with your meeting, I'll be waiting for you at the bar. Kay?" My voice comes out the chirpiest, peppiest imitation of a Cali airhead, and I couldn't be more pleased. Winking at the startled woman, I kiss Vadim right on his clenched cheek. "Don't work too hard."

Still grinning, I march to the bar where I promptly order my favorite vice and try not to die in utter shame. So the man who fucked my brains out—twice—is now interviewing marriage candidates right underneath my nose? I'm not jealous. Not in the slightest. After two sips of my wine, I'm not angry, either.

Especially when a hunky redhead in a dashing suit claims the stool next to me. "Is this seat taken?" he wonders, his blue eyes twinkling.

I clear my glass to the side and give him a more thorough once-over. "Not at all." He isn't bad for a last-minute option. He's certainly muscular enough. Who cares if his eyes aren't flashing with mystery, and his smile isn't dazzling?

I'm over the brooding, aloof thing, anyway.

To prove it, I stick out my hand, my expression simpering. "I'm—"

"Not taken, I hope," the man says, his gaze fixed beyond me.

"Huh?"

He chuckles, but there's a nervous quality to the sound. "Please tell me that the man staring daggers at me isn't your husband or something."

Husband, he says?

I laugh loudly as I extend my hand again. In a voice clear enough to be heard from the main lobby, I declare, "Oh no, I am *soooooooo* single. My name's Tiffy. What's yours?"

He rattles off a boring answer like Ben or Sam. Then he proceeds to spend the next ten minutes regaling me with tidbits of the stock exchange market. At the same time, I muster every ounce of control I possess not to turn around. And I don't. Even when an alarming warmth falls over my shoulder—the kind of pressure that could only belong to a masculine hand.

"*Baby*, I'm done with my meeting now, so you can stop provoking me. Kay?" a man purrs into my ear, his voice such a dead-on imitation of my Cali drawl that I do a doubletake. Dark eyes meet mine, sparkling with amusement—and something harder, promising punishment. "Tell the nice gent you're sorry for wasting his time," Vadim scolds, switching to his normal tone. Then he reaches into his pocket and withdraws a wad of cash that he offers to Ben, Sam—whoever—presumably as reimbursement for my second glass of wine.

Confused, the man takes the cash and backs off. "Sorry, man."

Once poor Ben or Sam has escaped the bar intact, I whirl to face the figure already perching onto the vacated stool beside me.

"Provoking you?" I parrot innocently and sip from my drink. "Is that what it's called when you're minding your own business, enjoying your time alone?" I pout and flutter my eyelashes. "My bed is so very big. I'll get lonely if I sleep in it by myself."

He frowns, his gaze dimming, and something that could be regret diminishes my feeling of triumph. No fair. He had to go and make things serious.

"Your wife candidate is gone?" I wonder, my tone slightly less nasty. After scanning the room, I don't find the woman anywhere. "Was she too brunette for your tastes? Too *'unpredictable'*?"

"Too jealous," he says in a deadpan tone. "She demanded to know why I was interviewing her when I have such a beautiful girlfriend." His frown lets me know that the words aren't his. Knowing that doesn't kill the fluttering butterflies that come to life in my stomach, though. "Had you not hung up on me, I would have further explained my motives," he adds, deliberately dangling a carrot before my nose.

Am I curious enough to take the bait? *No*, I decide, taking another sip of my wine. But then I remember how beautiful he looked, paired with a taller, more exotic looking woman, and a muscle in my jaw twitches.

"What motives could possibly explain interviewing marriage candidates?" I fold my hands neatly over my lap and feign interest. Internally, I'm struck by his appearance more than usual. The planes of his face seem bolder, his eyes darker. Even his hair looks glossier. Frowning, I try to pinpoint the source of the change, and then I find it—in addition to the ebony suit that I'm beginning to suspect is his signature look, a pop of color stands out in stark contrast. His shirt, a rich navy blue. I have a sudden flashback of me drunkenly informing him that blue is his color.

And it freaking is.

"Are you alright, Ms. Connors?" he wonders, his brows furrowing. At the same time, he strokes the edge of his collar, deliberately drawing my attention downward. "You seem distracted."

Rolling my eyes, I attempt to regroup. "Don't tell me the aloof bachelor is looking to settle down," I snipe. "Newsflash, that typically involves having to touch someone more often than giving them a kiss-off."

"In theory," he smoothly replies. "Luckily for me and my 'aloofness' this has nothing to do with romance whatsoever. I'm merely seeking a business arrangement."

"Oh?" I find myself inching closer to him while sneaking another sip from the rim of my glass. "A marriage of convenience?" I glance him over and nod with judgment. "You look like the type. You want your wife on call for public appearances with an agreement to freeze her eggs in case you desire an heir. No fucking required."

I sound so disappointed. Poor Vadim's future wife. He wouldn't want to endure the many, many, *many* sessions of sex it might take to conceive a baby. Halfway through, he'd close up out of nowhere, erect his iron wall and leave her high and dry. She'd be better off with a turkey baster. It would certainly provide more stable emotional support.

"You seem very interested in what duties I might desire in my wife," he points out.

I scoff and sip from my wine. Ignoring him would be the smart option—but I just can't help myself. "With your dazzling lack of imagination, I'm sure I have a pretty good idea already."

He chuckles, and I stiffen. Damn him, he can sound so carefree when he wants to. So…normal. So disarming.

"You have such a good idea of my intentions, and yet I doubt you would even make it through the interview process."

Low burn. I eye my drink and half-heartedly consider throwing it on him. Then I down it in one go and slam the empty glass onto the counter. Meeting his gaze directly, I fashion my most beautiful, charming smile. "Try me."

He stands without hesitation and approaches the table he left vacated. He moves so assuredly that I can't help feeling like a rabbit clumsily caught in a hunter's snare. I'd been so busy chasing my own tail that I didn't even see the trap coming.

"Change your mind?" Vadim calls without turning around.

I slink over to him, feigning disinterest with a bored sigh. To save face, I stall by circling around him before claiming the seat the brunette had occupied. My nostrils wrinkle, and I fight to stifle a frown. I can smell her perfume—cheap, knock-off designer.

"Ms. Connors, is it?" Vadim has a stack of papers placed before his spot. He leisurely rifles through them and looks up, eyeing me up and down. "I'm afraid your attire isn't at all appropriate," he scolds. "Did you even read the requirements?"

I squirm, unsure if he's joking or mocking. Probably both. It's so hard to tell with him. Biting my lip, I once again contemplate leaving—but the thought barely has time to form before I find myself leaning over the table instead. His quick glance downward reveals that my dirty trick hit its target—he definitely notices my cleavage, straining against the black silk of my dress. The effect is even more revealing if I arch my back in just the right angle.

So I do.

"I could go and change," I murmur innocently, deploying my sexy drawl. "Though you should loveeeeee this dress. *You* bought it."

"About that." He shifts, suddenly serious. "Your total came to—" he rattles off a number so insanely enormous that I instantly suppress it from my memory. "Would you like to repay me in a lump sum or in installments?"

I wrinkle my nose. Stealing from him was never my intention. Needling him a little? Totally. Still, even if it makes my throat go dry, I can't refuse him outright. "I do remember being promised a shopping spree in return for my accompanying you to ruin your brother's party—"

"That was for one dress," he clarifies, smoothing his finger along his collar. "Not four, a pair of shoes, a fur stole, a purse, two brooches and—"

"I'll return them, then," I say, dismissing him with a wave of my hand. "I kept the tags on. No harm, no foul."

"You won't." He laughs at the absurdity of such a proposal. "You had the driver circle around for hours until you found the exact store you wanted. Judging from your eventual tardiness, you spent even more time combing through each collection, picking your favorites. You may not be punctual, but I can tell you don't do things half-assed, either. To use that word, you so endeavor to abuse, you *love* those garments."

My heart races, panicked. I feel so personally insulted. So... known. He read me like a book, so expertly, he didn't even have to run his fingers through me to do it. No fair.

I try to salvage my pride with a toss of my hair and a bored sigh. "It's not like I could take them on the plane with me, anyway." *Lies.* I'd already run through the logistics hell of how to perfectly smuggle all four dresses, a purse, a pair of shoes, a fur stole, and two brooches into one of the customary wrapping boxes small enough to fit under my plane seat. Rather than admit defeat, I find ammunition to lob over the figurative net right back at him. "Most men would see the sex as more than enough payment."

He doesn't even flinch. "Yes. What was the rate I offered you? A grand for four hours." He extends one of his hands before him and eyes each finger. Reaching some internal conclusion, he looks up, jabbing his gaze right into mine. "It would take years for you to pay off such an investment."

Losing was never my forte. I suck at it, actually. Desperate to change the subject, I jab my finger at his stack of papers. "Ask me your stupid interview questions, then. I'm sure a man who can waste money on a fake wife can spare a few grand on some clothes." A few *hundred* grand, to be exact.

For whatever reason, he doesn't go in for the kill. Not yet, and my spine tingles with the painful reality that he has me by the balls this time.

"Do you have any relevant experience?" he wonders. Again, he utilizes that rich, unreadable tone that makes it hard to tell when he's serious or not. *Not,* I decide.

"I have seven years of it," I say, folding my hands onto the table. "All spent within an unhappy, loveless marriage. One could say I am an expert in the faking marital bliss arena."

He shuffles his documents, his expression unreadable. "What is the extent of your education?"

High school—the fancy boarding school variety, but with grades not worth bragging about. I find myself composing a different answer. "I taught Sunday school for five years. I'd make the good, wholesome breed of wife."

He raises an eyebrow, but I meet his skepticism shamelessly. I'm not lying. I'm not ashamed either. Teaching—even in the rather limited aspects of biblical commandments—is one of the few moments in my life with Jim I don't regret.

"Have you ever considered children?"

I wince. "Next question."

Something falls across his expression, hardening it. "No." He sets his pages aside and braces his hands over the table. "I'm afraid that question is non-negotiable."

I squirm. "And if I don't?"

He shrugs. But I can tell what will happen just from his rigid demeanor. He'll lose interest. Close up. Erect that stupid wall. Maybe I'm just too bored to let him retreat so soon?

"I *wanted* kids," I croak, hating how hoarse my voice sounds. "Once. My body had other plans. Besides, I'm fine with being single, and children mean no more frivolous expenses anyway. It's best for everyone."

"Money is no expense where I am concerned." In some ways, it resonates more like an insult than a simple statement. How dare

I even question? His hypothetical wife would have the best of both worlds, of course. A billion icy, brooding children and the wardrobe fit for a queen.

I hate her already.

"What is it you even do anyway?" I demand, scouring him with a more critical focus. Barely in his thirties, he couldn't have climbed too far up the corporate ladder. An heir of some kind? No. I grew up around boys with silver spoons stuck up their asses —though mine was shoved firmly in my mouth, so who am I to judge—but he doesn't fit the template. He's too cold in his dealings—a creature with nothing to prove to anyone. "A stockbroker?" I say, taking a guess out loud. "Venture capitalist?"

"To make it simple, let's say that I dabble in pharmaceuticals," he suggests. "A few strategic patents have made me a very, *very* wealthy man."

"Like?" I prod, curious enough to risk irritating him.

But he shrugs, unperturbed. "Are you familiar with Eingel Industries?"

I'm not. Still, it sounds prestigious enough to assuage my skepticism. "Smart as well as loaded—" I nod in approval. "I'm sure your future trophy wife will be very pleased."

"You have yet to ask me directly what it is I seek from my…wife."

Haven't I? I decide to cut the bullshit and take him up on the dare. "Why, oh, why would you want a wife, Vadim? Something tells me, it isn't to fuck."

"I seek a particular arrangement," he says cryptically. "To achieve that, I need to go through government officials, and in that capacity, I must present a certain…image to make the right impression."

"How did I know you wouldn't tell me outright," I mutter. "What do you want so badly that being a mere bachelor wouldn't get you?"

He shuffles his papers and elegantly tucks them within a leather briefcase he had placed by his feet. "I would tell you," he says without looking up, "had you actually passed your interview. I'm sorry to say that you failed."

Heat sears my cheeks. *Score: two Vadim, nil Tiffy.* Time to cut my losses and scurry away to lick my wounds.

"I'm leaving." I stand and turn my back to him, robbing him of the chance to inspect my reaction in full. "Enjoy your wife hunt. May you both find eternal bliss. I plan to find something *internal.*" I start for the doorway, forcing my chin high into the air. "Maybe I'll run into Sam in the lobby? I have time to kill before my flight, after all."

"His name was Joshua. And you can wave to him on your way upstairs," Vadim replies. "Because you won't have time to engage him in conversation."

My steps falter. "And why is that?"

"Because you need to change into another one of your stolen dresses. I've decided to take you to dinner."

My mind reels. He's *decided.* It sounds so damn insulting that I puff up instantly incensed. And at the same time, it seems so damn intriguing. So damn…commanding. First spanking. Now, this. The man is insane.

But damn, I may love it.

"I don't remember agreeing to anything of the sort?" I crane my neck to eye him from over my shoulder.

And I instantly regret it. Holy crap. His eyes blaze, a muscle in his throat jerking freely.

"You'll come," he says. That's it. As if he's so damn sure I wouldn't dare refuse. It's only when he finally deigns to eye his watch that I realize I've stood here all this time, gaping at him open-mouthed. "I'll give you an hour to change," he says as though bestowing some precious gift upon me. "Wear something I haven't seen you in before. I'll meet you in the lobby."

"You are so full of shit," I blurt incredulously.

He merely inclines his head as if considering the phrase. "I've filled you as well," he finally counters in that deep, relentless murmur. "But it wasn't with shit, was it?"

My mouth falls open even wider, and I have to make a mental note to close it. Turning on my heel, I storm for the main lobby. Before decorum can rob me of the gall, I stick up my middle finger in a princess-style wave as I go. "Fuck off, Vadim."

But damn him. The way he said filled. It does strange things to my head and conjures dangerous, explicit memories. Like him swelling inside me on the verge of release—and then the eventual sensation of being flooded by him. Consumed by him.

CHAPTER ELEVEN

I sway on my way into an elevator, and I nearly run into the suite in a desperate bid to escape thoughts of him. Dinner, he says? Hell no. I'm going to pack for my flight, order a million wake up calls, and do whatever it takes to ensure that I make it on time. I'm going to…

Scream and race out of the room as if electrocuted. My heart pounds as I warily tiptoe back inside, unwilling to believe my eyes.

My first coherent thought is that the bastard stalled me on purpose, knowing all along that someone was in my room unloading boxes upon boxes placed throughout the master suite. A stack lies before the bed and more dominate the glass dining table by the window. Not just any boxes either, but a classic, iconic black box wrapped in signature white ribbon…

Chanel. So much Chanel that I fear I'm hallucinating. *Obscene* amounts of Chanel. He must have spent a literal fortune. Either that or he's playing a sick, awful joke at my expense.

So, of course, it's the latter.

Sighing, I fight to control any excitement that may be bubbling beneath my skin as I approach the nearest stack and lift one of the boxes. It's heavy enough to prove that it's not filled with air, at least. But when I peek inside…

I sink to my knees and wind up cooing over the most beautiful purse I've ever seen. It matches the ebony dress I discover next. And a pair of similar shoes, and then a collection of delicate jewelry. Jackets. More shoes. More purses.

And then it clicks. The bastard bought the spring collection. The most iconic, eye-catching pieces, to boot. Gosh, just last month, I'd drooled over the lineup, trying to talk myself into flirting with bankruptcy just to buy a single purse. Maybe a pair of shoes?

In person, every piece is more beautiful than I could have ever imagined. All I can do is strip my black dress and try on a new, light pink one with worshiping reverence. In a daze, I discover a full-length mirror on the closet door, and I admire myself from every angle.

Then I try on another ensemble. And another. Another.

It quickly becomes apparent that he didn't settle for just teasing me with a few new dresses. He bought entire outfits down to the last finishing detail. I recognize more than half from the runway, and something he said to me echoes in my brain as I model yet another gorgeous dress—wear something *different,* he commanded me in reference to his dinner.

The bastard.

I get lost in the task of trying to find which dress—of many—I'm aching to test drive first. The pink? The blue? An innocent sheer white?

I'm barely halfway through my options when the door to the suite opens, and a lanky, smug bastard strolls in.

"How did I know that this would be the cause of your delay?" He gestures to the mess of tissue paper and cardboard coating nearly every inch of the floor. His neutral expression doesn't quite match the surliness conveyed by his tone. He's not entirely angry, just amused.

And what he said finally registers in my brain. *Delay?*

Only now do I realize that it's nearly pitch-black outside. I'd turned on a few lights to better illuminate the details of each garment, so I barely noticed. Concerning his dinner date, I'm about four hours too late.

I try to apologize, I think, but all I manage to muster is a pained groan as I model another black dress and promptly fall in love. Thinking quickly, I skip through the minefield of clothing and grab a checkered style boy bag from the chaos. When slung over my shoulder, it completes the outfit so perfectly I gasp, and my eyes roll back into my head.

"You truly feel this way about a few items of clothing?" Vadim wonders. He's seated on the bed, watching me, his gaze unreadable.

"Clothing?" I sound so horrified by such a dismissive term. "This is *art.*" But even as my heart soars with affection for every beautiful piece, my inner bitch has to dampen my mood. "But I can't keep it." It nearly kills me to even suggest as much out loud. *Kills.*

"Is that so?" His eyes flicker dangerously as he blinks without an ounce of mercy. "I could return it…"

"You should." I last all of five seconds before I break down shamelessly. "No, please! I have nothing to wear, thanks to you —" My suitcase is somewhere in an abandoned hotel room back in Cali. Considering that most of that clothing consists of conservative holdovers from my life with Jim, I'm more than ready for an upgrade. Biting my lip, I twirl and sigh in admiration of how amazing this dress alone makes me look. Even he has to appreciate the effect. And after all, I deserve a reward for putting up with him. He's been so darn mean.

"What will you give me for it?" His low, husky tone makes me swallow hard.

Too terrified to look at him, I observe my reflection more intently than ever.

"I would offer you my body, but we both know that you aren't particularly interested in that." I should leave it there and salvage what little I have of my pride by throwing every last item in the trash. Reflexively, my fingers grasp the strap of the purse, but I can't seem to budge. "What would you want?" I finally demand.

"I want you to accompany me to dinner," he says.

"Is that it?" I frown at his tone. The audible hesitation doesn't match the ominous way he uttered that word. *Dinner.* Curious, I crane my head back to peek at him.

He's staring into space, his mouth more tense than the smirk I'm used to.

"Dinner," he repeats. "With Milton…and my brother."

"Oh." I look away and finger the skirt of my dress. Even an idiot could catch the reluctance lurking beneath his level tone. "Well, I... Wait, that dinner isn't until next week!"

"Monday, in fact," he clarifies. "A timeframe that I'm sure gives you more than enough opportunities to utilize my bank account in your quest for revenge."

I whirl on him, hands on my hips. "Pray tell, Vadim, you aren't trying to keep me here yet another week?" I sound playfully alarmed, but inside I'm panicking. Could I survive another week in this man's orbit? One look at his quick, devious smile, and I have my answer.

Hell no.

"You can keep the Chanel," I say a bit more seriously this time. I carefully shimmy out of my dress, fold it, and return it to one of the boxes. "Now get out of my bed. I need to get up early tomorrow."

I stroll toward him, vaguely aware of the fact that I'm butt naked —underwear, ironically, hasn't been a priority during any of my few shopping sprees, and my only pairs are in said lost luggage. Circling around to the side of the bed opposite him, I make a show of yawning and lie on my side with my back to him.

"Goodnight—"

"And here I was assuming that the entire Chanel spring collection was the way to your heart."

I scoff. "I would have to be an idiot to let you anywhere near my heart." I'm startled by just how genuinely I mean that. Already something in my chest feels...off. I don't care what it takes— tomorrow, I leave.

"Nothing might change your mind?" he wonders, still so deceptively neutral. A different woman might make the mistake of assuming he's bored, even. Just prolonging this conversation to kill time. But I'm beginning to realize that time is the one commodity Mr. Vadim Gorgoshev doesn't spend frivolously.

And that icky feeling in my chest grows tenfold.

"No," I say smoothly. Then my brain catches up and has the nerve to contradict me. "Fine. What might change my mind? I want a straight answer from you for once. I want to know your secrets. And—" I wince as my stomach growls loudly enough for him to hear. "I'm hungry."

When he doesn't reply, I roll over and rise onto my knees, only to find him seated close to the phone, a glossy black brochure in hand. "Room service?" he inquires, switching to his deeper, more professional baritone. "*Parlez-vous Français? Très bien.*"

He presumably proceeds to order from the menu, only he's speaking entirely in French. Given that up until now, everyone in this damn hotel has spoken nothing but unaccented English, I recognize the act for the power play it truly is. A display purely meant to disarm me.

Finished, he sets the phone down and then inclines his head as if I'm the one intruding upon his stolen room. "You were saying?"

I want to be angry. Deviously, spitefully angry. Something about him makes me more reckless instead. So it's mind games he wants to play?

I shuffle toward him, still on my knees, and then I shamelessly drape myself over him from behind, bringing my mouth near his ear. He stiffens predictably—score one for me—but an answering shiver ripples down my spine, and the score evens out.

I love how solid he feels against me. So strong. I can lean all my weight against him, and I have no doubt that he can handle it.

Snap out of it, Tiffy.

"*Baby*," I murmur, adopting my ditzy wifey drawl from earlier. "I might consider staying if you tell me all of your deepest, darkest secrets."

"Like?" he wonders.

I swallow. Ask him something profound and personal? My tongue has a different aim in mind. "Why do you have your penis pierced?"

We both glance down to the center of his slacks. Is that a slight bulge I see? My cheeks heat, and I'm not sure if I enjoy the idea that he may like feeling me against him as much as I do. Or, it could be a trick of the light.

"Why? Control," he says simply. "To prove that I alone can exert ownership over my body."

I frown. It's a surprisingly deep and profound answer. I figure most men in the same position would mention something about wanting better orgasms. Intrigued, I shift around him to straddle his lap, spreading my legs directly over that suspicious bulge. Persistent heat firmly nudges my core, and I flinch in response. Not a trick of the light, after all.

Fighting to stay focused, I rise up just enough so that I can look down on him, and I quirk my lips into my own mischievous smile. "Do you think I should get my clit pierced, baby? I, too, am known for my exemplary self-control."

A muscle in his jaw twitches even as his dark eyes remain carefully blank. "I don't think you could handle the pain, *baby*."

"Oh?" *Bastard.* I lower myself hard, relishing in the low grunt that rips from his throat. His hands capture my hips automatically though he doesn't guide my movements—deliberately, I suspect with an internal giggle. My first aim is to change that. "I can handle anything," I insist while rocking my hips to tease that bulge further.

Within seconds, however, the tables turn. Needling him becomes less important than feeling him. Moisture dampens my inner thighs and at the back of my mind, I know it's shameless to tease him, when I could wind up ruining his expensive clothes in the process. But logic melts away like tissue paper against the waves of pleasure just grinding on him inspires. If I shift in the right direction, the friction of his pants scrapes over my clit. It's brief, fiery bliss. A little wiggle in the other direction, and the sensation is enhanced tenfold.

And I'm not the only one loving this, it seems.

His eyelids flutter, his jaw tightening by the second. A hint of something dangerous flickers across his irises, gone before I even have the sense to fear it. Sense being the operative word.

He feels so damn good. My thoughts dissipate, and what little remain turn to sex. What it would feel like if he fucked me from this position. How his piercing would feel pressing against the innermost parts of me. Each devious thought seems to take control of my hips, making them move faster. Slower.

As if from far away, I register a sudden knock on the door of the suite, followed by Vadim's surprisingly guttural command, "Come in."

"H-Huh?" I vaguely register the door opening before a tall man in a suit strolls in, a silver tray balanced on one hand while he holds a bottle of wine in the other. Our unfortunate room service deliverer.

He takes one look at me—straddling Vadim completely naked—and nearly drops both items onto the damn floor. Not to mention that the sea of partially opened Chanel boxes makes the room a hell he's forced to navigate like some weird, fashion-focused game of twister. Finally, he makes it to the dining table and unloads his burden before he practically hops back to the entrance of the suite.

"Add a grand to the tab for the gratuity," Vadim says as the man bows and closes the door.

"Mean!" I grind on him mercilessly, desperate to ruin his fancy smanshy pants by way of payback. My traitorous body makes that task ten times easier to accomplish—the tailor-made fabric is already soaked. My brain is in la-la land, and I'm too far gone to stop. I could come like this, I realize happily. I wiggle my hips in the hopes of spurring that inevitability on faster. He might have the last laugh, but at least I'd salvage something from this. Something I suspect will be well worth the hassle. Tempting heat creeps through my belly, spurring me on. I'm so close already…

And right when I'm on the very edge, he grips my hips, wrenching me off of him.

"No!" I claw at his shoulders, trying to find my way back onto his lap.

I'm no match. Utilizing effortless strength, he stands, keeping me at bay with a single grip on my arm. Then he pivots. I land on my back, staring up at him stunned as he rips the belt from his slacks and tosses it aside. My mouth waters when he unfastens his pants next, freeing his cock. It's more than just a little hard now, pulsing and erect, his piercing gleaming.

I spread my legs, alarmed by how his eyes fixate on me in response. He's anything but disinterested. Even the thought of having him touch me makes all of my logical brain malfunction. The needy whore takes over.

"Please..." I arch my hips, presenting myself to him. "Please. Please—"

An uncharacteristic grunt rips from him. Tearing off his suit jacket, he mounts the bed and grabs my thigh, yanking me closer. My heart pounds as my ass comes precariously close to slipping off the edge of the mattress.

Before I can even fall, he catches my thigh, positioning himself against me. Those dark eyes find mine, flashing and furious. Have I pushed poor Vadim to his limits again?

Good. I writhe, stroking myself up and down his length, feeling him strain even as he grits his teeth. The reigns of his restraint are stretched thin, I suspect. Seconds from snapping entirely.

So I do the good, respectful thing and palm his hips, sinking my nails in.

"*Merde!*" He bucks, entering me so mindlessly deep that I lose track of everything but the need to drive him deeper. Take more.

I beg for him, slurring each request in increasingly explicit tones that would make me blush in my right mind. "Fuck me. Yes. So deep. Please!"

I come off the mattress, nearly climbing up his body just to enhance every thrust. My moans drip into his ear, my nails grazing whatever parts of him I can reach.

"So good. So good. So good—"

Suddenly, he rears back and feels along the mattress until he finds something long… His belt. I stiffen, alarm battling the lust turning my brain to mush. "W-What are you…"

He takes my hands, bringing them together. Then he wraps the length of the belt around them both and ties it tight, binding me. Restraining me.

And the fact of him robbing me of the ability to even touch him does something weird to my head. I'm boiling. He grates out another foreign curse, rocking his hips as if to stave off his release —but he can't. He's thickening inside me, setting off a chain reaction that boils my blood and has me screaming. Never have I ever come so hard in my life. My toes curl, my back arching off the bed, my body rippling around him like a vice.

It goes on and on and on. When I finally come down, I'm murmuring senseless praise that makes him shudder.

"So good. So good. Please more. Please. Please."

He withdraws from me so violently it hurts. I moan, struck dumb with shock only to find myself shoved onto my stomach as his weight pins me from behind. Again, he slams in, still rock hard.

But this angle…

Everything feels enhanced to the nth degree, and I cry out throatily in pleasure. It's like he knows me from the inside out. How to create the most toe-curling friction. What spots to press. How to move. How to stop, leaving me quaking on the very edge of sanity.

Just when I'm about to tip over, he hisses out something too grated for me to interpret. A curse? His hand falls over my ass, squeezing hard. Then he withdraws and then rapidly brings his palm down, resulting in a stinging slap.

Again.

Again.

"Never," he snarls in a tone I've yet to hear from him. "Never wanted to chastise a woman. But you…" Another smack makes me writhe into the contours of his hand, extending the contact. "You demand to be punished."

"So punish me," I blurt. Or at least, I would if I was in control of my brain enough to adequately transfer the command to my mouth. I moan instead, rocking into his next tentative thrust.

I feel like I'm burning alive.

My only salvation is the relief that comes from release, and I slavishly chase it. Eventually, he regains his brutal rhythm, driving me across the mattress with each wrenching thrust. Ultimately my upper body is left leaning over the edge of the bed, and I'm staring dazedly at the floor as he finally groans and his cock thrums against my battered walls.

Somehow, I manage to twist around to watch him, and I promptly rocket to cloud nine all over again. With his head thrown back, throat cording around a groan, he looks so beautiful it hurts. His hooded eyes meet mine, and I'm shocked at what I find swirling within them. Pleasure mixed with hesitant relief.

Like he didn't think it was possible to feel *this* good.

This free.

Like sex—despite his obvious prowess—is a novel experience to him, he's only recently discovered.

In this brief second, he looks at me like he's never come this hard or for this long…

For anyone.

And I know as a logical part of me reforms and urges a warning that I need to get my ass back to California. As soon as possible.

He is the most dangerous man I've ever met—and I'm enjoying that way too much.

CHAPTER TWELVE

"I love this wine!" I brandish my third glass at Vadim and open my mouth for the forkful of pasta he amusedly shoves into it. "And I love this food," I murmur in ecstasy, my eyes threatening to roll.

We're in bed again. Together. A bad idea, but I'm drunk, so who cares?

He's naked, lying beside me with a plate of lukewarm pasta between us, and a bottle of the amazing wine propped up on a pillow nearby. I wiggle my sore limbs, stretching as I watch him sample his own much smaller bite of pasta.

"You have such a beautiful mouth," I gush mournfully. "What a shame you won't get to use it on me before I leave."

I'm surprisingly devastated by the idea. To drown my sorrows, I sip more of my wine and distract myself with the contours of his abs instead.

"You're perfect," I tell him, brushing my fingers along his right pec. "It's unfair you're so beautiful."

His eyes cloud over, stormy and distant. "And you are still so affectionate after a glass or two of wine," he remarks, his annoyance palpable.

"Why do you hate when I praise you?" I drain the rest of my glass and set it aside. Then I prop my chin on my fist and observe him critically. "Every time I say anything nice about you, you get so surly and mean."

"What is praise, and what is…leverage?" he counters.

"Ah, I get it." I roll my eyes knowingly. "The big bad rich, handsome billionaire has become so jaded to compliments and the schmoozing of others. He can no longer trust who truly wants him or his money. Am I correct?"

He nods in capitulation. "Though it is not always money."

"Hmm." I stroke my chin, mulling over the sheer depths of his paranoia. To live as such with a body like his. It must be hell. "I can't speak for anyone else, but typically when a woman climaxes on your cock while screaming about how good you feel, she most likely means it."

It's the wine making me so tactless. But why stop now? I fumble for the bottle and add pointedly, "Since I'm never going to see you again after tomorrow, allow me to get it all out now. I love how you look. So sexy but so understated, requiring a second glance to register the full effect. And—" I try to pour myself a fresh glass and wind up spilling more wine onto myself than anything. Sighing, he's forced to assist me, manipulating the bottle with his much steadier touch. In triumph, I take another sip and settle against a mound of displaced pillows. "I love your mouth. I love your eyes, especially—I never know what you're thinking. I love when you spank me…" I trail off as I notice him staring far more intently than before. "And, I love your voice. I really love your cock. It's perfection. And I *love* your piercing—"

"Enough to copy me?" he wonders, swiping his finger along my belly.

I reflexively clamp my knees together at first. Then, emboldened by another sip of wine, I spread them, revealing every inch of the flesh in question. At the back of my mind, I marvel at how comfortable I feel in front of him. I panic at it. I felt dirty in anything less than a conservative negligee around Jim. He made me feel as if his lust was my sin. But Vadim?

He makes lust feel as heady as alcohol, mine alone to enjoy. To get drunk on.

And it feels so good to get drunk.

"You would pierce this?" he wonders, eyeing my anatomy skeptically.

"I would," I boast. "For a price."

He frowns, unimpressed. "You would mutilate yourself just to please another?"

"Oh, I've been curious about it," I admit with a shrug. "I've heard it can make you orgasm like that—" I snap my fingers for emphasis. "But I'm so horny that I could make myself come while thinking about a wet paper bag. But you? I have a hunch that you would *love* to see me pierced."

Not that he ever would because I'm leaving in the morning. He knows I'm going. Even as his eyes take on a thoughtful, dangerous gleam, he knows it…

"I'd let you have a say in every part of it," I add, casually sipping more wine while playing with fire. "The size. Placement. I'd even let you pick the metal—"

"Silver," he says absently. "Of the highest quality. And you seem perfectly suited for a VCH."

"Oh?" I lift an eyebrow and run my tongue along the rim of my glass. So much for his aversion to kink. He sounds fairly knowledgeable in this arena all of a sudden—too knowledgeable. A part of me can't help wondering if clitoral piercings is a subject he regularly tackles with his one-night stands. Or just me. For instance, if he only started researching the topic not long after our very first meeting when I drunkenly expressed interest in it? A dangerous thought that requires another tasting of wine to wash it down.

"What's a VCH?" I ask, turning to a much less risky topic.

"A vertical clitoral hood piercing," he says, his gaze flashing and devious once more. "It's well known for increasing stimulation during sex."

I suck in a breath, intrigued. But then I remember the caveat making this entire conversation moot. "What a shame that I'm leaving tomorrow—" In six hours, to be exact, judging from the flashing numbers on the console by the TV. "If only you were nicer to me. We could have had so much fun." In very real disappointment, I down the rest of my glass in one go.

"Hypothetically speaking, what would your price be?"

"Hmm." I cast him an appraising glance, though I already know my answer. I've been thinking of it obsessively ever since the first damn time he slapped my ass. Even now, I'm growing wet at the prospect of it and just how much I'll be denied when it comes to him and sex. Therefore, I have no guilt in blurting out the truth. "My price? That would be *you*, Mr. Vadim. I'd want you to—"

Both of his eyebrows go up in shock as I proceed to lay out a detailed list of all of my fantasies when it comes to kink. All. Of. Them. Bondage. Being pilloried. Much more "chastisement." I mention the one time I briefly considered nipple clamping but chickened out. Orgies. Exhibition. Being blindfolded and gagged. And then a whole list of items so X-rated I immediately block them from my memory the second I utter them.

By the time I finish, Vadim actually looks shocked. Not merely amused. Shook.

Score two for Tiffy. Utterly pleased with myself, I lean back further against the cushions supporting me, displaying the breasts that I just admitted I'd wanted clamped, teased, and tormented.

"We would have to wait to do the really fun stuff until after the piercing healed, of course," I add, taking this ball and running far with it. "That could take… I don't know—"

"Four to eight weeks," he supplies. "About the same length of time it would take to special order the apparatuses you so cleverly described. Even if I paid the rush fee."

Again, he sounds far too knowledgeable on the subject. Even I know when to back down at the last minute.

"Yes, well, it will never happen." I lean over to place my glass and plate on the nightstand. Then I proceed to shimmy beneath the luxurious blankets. With my back to him, I yawn for real and make a show of closing my eyes. "Nighty night. See you again, never. Try not to make too much noise on your way out. I'm a very—"

"Light sleeper," he finishes, but I can't escape the sense that it sounds more mocking than insightful. Like he knows some delicious secret I don't regarding my sleep.

Back off, Tiffy.

"Night!" I slam a blanket over my head and settle down in earnest. Before I drift off, I send up a prayer that I'll wake up in time to catch my flight. *Amen.*

And that once I land in California, I'll magically forget all about Vadim and his kink.

Amen, amen.

A girl can dream.

CHAPTER THIRTEEN

I wake up with roughly two hours to get dressed and hustle to the airport—which is the good news. The bad news is that I wake up so content that I think I'm in a dream at first. A dream so sensual and relaxing that it couldn't possibly be real. It stars my naked body and someone's hand on my ass. A hand composed of slim fingers that involuntarily stroke me every now and again as if its owner can't keep his hands off me even in his sleep.

That's why I woke up. I'm so damn horny that my brain couldn't cope, instinctively knowing that something is horribly wrong. Because the hand is very real, I realize as I tentatively arch my back and said fingers grope me in response. Not to mention that the owner's smell is so damn signature that there is no mistaking his identity.

It's *Vadim's* hand.

Crap. I blink my eyes open to the darkened hotel room. Someone drew the courtesy blinds closed after I went to bed.

That same person, no doubt, rearranged the pillows and neatly tucked the blankets over us both. My mouth drops open. The bastard had the sheer gall to climb beneath them with me as if we were a normal couple after a normal night of normal sex.

The worst part is how damn beautiful he looks. Watching him deeply asleep should be a crime against humanity. He looks so… vulnerable for once, with his dark lashes fanning his cheekbones and his curls framing his face like a corrupted halo. But that vulnerability lasts up until the moment my gaze falls over his mouth, still fixed in that surly, mistrustful line. Even in his sleep, the man has his wall up.

Get out of here, Tiffy. I tear my gaze away from him and creep into the bathroom. There I take the quickest whore bath imaginable, and then I find my way through the dark to fish out the one outfit I refuse to leave behind—a black, red, and white checkered tweed suit and skirt ensemble with a frothy white blouse to go underneath. For good measure, I find a beautiful black clutch too incredible to risk abandoning. Then I tiptoe toward the door of the suite in a pair of black block heels.

A sigh of relief escapes me once I clear the minefield of clothing boxes. Paces from the door, I eagerly reach out for the handle, and I'm home free.

Until a deep, sexily husky voice rings out, "I'm afraid to inform you that your flight has been canceled."

I whirl around to find Vadim still in bed, a lazy smirk playing over his lips, visible even in the dark. His eyes practically glow with amusement, and I flick the nearest light switch, robbing him of the mystery of shadow to hide behind. The action backfires—gosh, he looks more mouthwatering in the dim glow cast by one of the bedside lamps. The sight of his bare chest makes me groan—the gleaming, chiseled panes practically demand further exploration. With my fingers. With my mouth.

I shake my head to clear the thoughts, blinking to refocus. "W-Why? I mean, how do you even know that?"

He extends his arms and casually laces his fingers together behind his head, leaning back against the pillows. "Because I took the liberty of canceling it."

Shock makes me sway, all tension of my potential escape dashed. I feel along the wall until I reach a leather-backed chair and collapse onto it.

"Why?"

"Why?" He inclines his head, an eyebrow raised. "I don't typically allow people to steal from me."

I scoff. "You don't own me." But he does own this dress. And this purse. And these shoes… Clearing my throat, I rush to add, "And you can bill me for the clothing. I'll pay it off."

Internally, I'm screaming. Realistically I *could* pay it off…if I sold my body for a few years into sexual slavery. Even my trust fund wouldn't cut it, nor my alimony. Theoretically, I could always ask my parents to cover maybe a teensy, weensy fraction—a few grand at least. But the guilt would eat me alive, so that's a no.

Sexual slavery it is.

"Money was not the agreed upon price," Vadim says, his tone scolding. My ass smarts in memory of his "punishment," and I hate myself. How is it possible for someone to switch from icy cool to sexy dark so easily? "I will take my payment in full," he adds as if aware of his effect on me.

"Payment," I grouse. "Dinner with your brother? Are you that afraid of going alone?"

What I intend to sound taunting lands with a thud when he nods.

"Yes," he says unapologetically. "I am. Maxim and I can rarely occupy the same space without…unpleasantries."

Minus the one night I accompanied him, and we scored two presents out of it. Sighing, I lean forward and tap my chin as if mulling over the prospect—which I'm not. A week is far too long to stay here, away from home. Far too long to stay within the orbit of such a dangerous man. I've already lost my brain around him—twice. No siree can that happen again.

"You're considering," he remarks as if reading my mind. "Tell me what will put you over the edge."

I grit my teeth, still contemplating the idea of running down to the front lobby and begging the concierge to find me any flight leaving within the hour to anywhere but here. If only his voice didn't make the demand sound so damn tempting.

"I'll need underwear," I point out. "I mean, I would, *if* I were staying—which I'm not."

He nods. "Fair enough."

"But not just any underwear… Lingerie. French-style from Atelier Noir. An assortment of course. Bras, panties, and full sets." Gosh, I can barely keep the excited squeal from my voice. Designer to the rich and famous, the items from Atelier Noir are legendary in both style and price. I once made the mistake of looking up the cost of a bra and panty set I'd admired in a magazine and promptly fell into a weeklong despair at the price.

"Done," he says. A devious part of me wants to drop an average price point of the garments and watch him squirm—but the longer I observe him, the more I suspect that he already knows the cost and then some. Either way, he's prepared to pay it.

"You drop obscene amounts of money on your one-night stand, and yet you clam up the second she says anything nice about you." I raise a skeptical eyebrow, crossing my legs.

"Clothing, money, and even lingerie is a physical exchange," he explains, sounding like some stuffy professor—not that I had ever gone to one college class to know the difference. "Compliments, on the other hand? Praise? Those are delivered with only one goal in mind. Manipulation." He's staring off into space, no doubt glowering at the memory of all the prior women who dared to compliment him.

"So cynical!" I lean forward and eye him with renewed scrutiny. "I've changed my mind. You know what will make me stay? You praise *me*. Something nice and personal—you've called me beautiful before," I add before he can say as much. "But that doesn't count."

"Why not?"

I frown, uncomforted by the answer. "Because it's not a real compliment," I say. "It's an assessment. You can call me beautiful, but it doesn't require any personal engagement on your part. I want you to dig deep, Vadim. For instance…" Licking my lips, I sweep my gaze along him and settle over his waist. "I've told you that you have a beautiful cock, that I enjoy it—but have I told you why? It's so damn good that I think you've adopted it as your primary personality. Dick."

He chuckles, and I inhale at the genuine sound. "Praise. That is all it will take for you to stay?"

"Well, I do need new underwear." I glance forlornly at the brand-new, priceless skirt I'm already in danger of ruining. Lately, sex has been on my brain more often than not—making up for lost time and all that—but never to this extent. Being around him has me in a perpetual state of arousal, and I hate myself. "But yes. Offer me a real, heartfelt compliment, and I'll stay. Until Monday. After that, you're allowing me the use of your private plane to go back to Cali so that you can't 'cancel' any more commercial flights."

He frowns, looking surlier than ever.

"I can start, if you want?" I say sweetly. "Watch and learn—I love your cock. I love how you fuck when you lose yourself in the moment. I love it when you slap me on the—"

"The things you say." His frown deepens, his brow furrowing in aggravation. "Am I really to believe that you were a Sunday school teacher?"

"Amen," I say solemnly. "But whether you believe me or not doesn't matter to me. I don't spend my life concerned with the intentions of others like you do."

Minus, of course, those of the dangerous, enticing billionaire who toys with me like a bored owner tossing his hyper puppy a bone every now and again.

"Now give me what I want," I prod. "Or I'll go to the airport right now and find a pilot to screw. *That* will get me a ride home, I'm sure—"

"Since you're already dressed, we'll do breakfast instead of dinner," Vadim says. He shoves the covers back and stands.

And my brain short-circuits.

Unsurprisingly, he's still naked, and my eyes feast upon his body when glimpsed in full. His cock is breathtaking, of course, stiff with morning wood—but his ass. Damn, his ass. I nearly groan out loud as he turns around and bends to pick up his discarded clothing from the floor.

"Is that agreement, I wonder?" he asks without turning around.

"H-Huh?" I blink, struck dumb. The man was crafted by the Devil himself. Slender and lean, the one part of him that isn't solid muscle, is balanced on top of his muscular thighs. Plump and firm, it looks so damn squeezable that I have to clench my hands into fists just to stop from reaching out.

"I asked if you were going to be agreeable and join me for breakfast or if you were going to insist I jump through some kind of hoop first?" he says, turning to face me, his clothing slung over one arm.

Dick.

"Praise me," I demand, rising to my feet as well. "Or I'm leaving. I mean it—"

"You…" He eyes me as if hunting for something he can find to compliment me on. When the seconds tick by, heat sears my cheeks.

"Well, don't try too hard," I snap. "You might give yourself an aneurysm—"

"Your smile is…decent," he says finally. "Satisfied?"

"Thanks," I croon, displaying the smile in question. "With a little bit more training, I'll have you an expert in bedroom talk."

For his next conquest, of course. Because by then, I'll be in Cali crawling under another businessman. Or maybe a doctor.

"I need to change." He strolls to the door, unabashedly bare. "Preferably before you attempt to sneak away, thus committing theft. Though I am sure you are above such devious actions?"

I shiver as he passes me, and it takes everything I have to keep from ogling his ass a second time.

"I'm not," I admit. "The second you leave, I'm running headlong to the lobby. Try and stop me."

"Is that so?" He eyes me from over his shoulder, his smirk firmly in place. Casually he dons his shirt and suit jacket and then slips into his pants. The only missing item is his belt, which I think is lost in the bed somewhere. Rather than hunt for it, he enters the hallway, and I follow him, more than ready to attempt my escape.

I expect him to head for the elevator, or maybe the stairs. Anything but across the hall and casually fish a keycard from his pocket. One swipe, and the door opens.

"You rented out the suite next to mine?" I stammer open-mouthed.

He enters the suite, and his voice reaches back to me. "You mean —I rented out two suites adjacent to each other? Then yes. The fact that you manage to occupy one serves only as a testament to your remarkable ability to take from me what you may."

"Oh, really?" I storm after him, shocked to find a suite every bit as spacious as mine. The only difference is the obsessive, painful level of neatness that I suspect goes far beyond the hotel cleaning services. There isn't so much as a used napkin lying around, and all of his clothing appears to be neatly unpacked and stored within the walk-in closet. He enters it and proceeds to undress while eyeing his options.

I shimmy past him and gain an up-close look at what essentials a billionaire might think to pack in his travel wardrobe. Lots of black, for one. A multitude of simple, but crisply tailored suits and a boring arrangement of ties. Though professional attire isn't all that I find dangling from wooden hangers. Tucked at the very back is an array of insultingly plain sweatshirts when compared to the quality of everything else.

"A gym rat?" I suspect out loud. That would certainly explain his remarkably fit shape. Biting my lower lip, I flick through the nearest selection of suits. Tucked amongst all the black is a collection in a deep, rich shade of navy, and I'm too tempted to resist.

"Don't tell me your style has changed within the space of five seconds," Vadim murmurs as I strip the suit from the hanger. "I must say that I'm curious as to how a masculine style would look on you."

I suck in a breath but push the thought out of my mind instantly. Wearing his clothing is way too intimate. "Wear this," I demand, whirling around to shove the suit at him. "Eww. Not that!" I playfully smack his hand away as he reaches for an ebony selection instead. "This one."

I hold the jacket up to his chest and instantly regret the selection. "Maybe not."

Like a shark sensing blood in the water, he snatches the garments from me and tugs them on as I watch, increasingly terrified by the overall effect.

Damn, damn, damn. Blue is so his color—to an alarming degree. It enhances the darkness reflecting in his eyes and brilliantly plays off the paleness of his chin. The only thing that could possibly enhance the look more is…

I scan the space for it, and my eyes fall over a tie organizer hanging on the opposite side of the closet. Sure enough, shoved at the very bottom in an array of muted colors is a navy one made of silk. My fingers shake as I loop it around Vadim's neck.

"So much better," I confess. "You're far too handsome to avoid color."

"Is that so?" He's frowning as he adjusts the tie, deftly tying it. "Will you make me buy myself a wardrobe next?"

I flinch at the surly tone, but he presents a tempting possibility. "Maybe," I say, my voice distant as I picture how he'd look in red. My throat goes dry.

"So…breakfast." Forging a change in subject, I slip past him and re-enter the bedroom. "Where are you taking me?"

I steel myself for some insanely expensive restaurant or a McDonalds—knowing him, either option is within the realm of possibility, chosen primarily to catch me off guard.

"Downstairs," he says, surprising me. "I have a standing reservation. It will, however, serve as a business meeting as well."

As if to demonstrate as much, he crosses to a briefcase placed beside the entrance and lifts it. "After you."

"Business?"

He doesn't give me an explanation as I follow him out into the hall. We take the elevator down to the lobby, and within minutes, we're herded to a beautiful table in the back of an elegant French restaurant.

"Are you French?" I ask him as I claim the seat across from him. I notice that the menu is in French and paired with his display from last night, I think he enjoys flaunting his bilingualism before me.

"My mother was," he admits, opening his menu to scan the pages. "And it is my preferred culture of the many I grew up immersed in."

"Military brat?" I say, taking a guess. He certainly has the stone-cold emotional range of someone who grew up with a hard ass, drill sergeant parent.

He looks away, and his gaze turns distant. "No. Not quite."

"You don't like to talk about your childhood," I surmise. "That could be a good thing. Mine was so boringly typical that there isn't much to talk about."

"Oh?" Real interest flashes across his features.

"My dad was an investment banker," I admit. "My mother was a glorified housewife—but damn good at it. My uncle Conroy runs one of the largest vineyards in the country, and I had the typical, milk toast, country club, basic bitch white girl upbringing."

And there is no shame in that.

"But you were married…" He busies himself with pouring water from a pitcher into two glasses, but I sense that he's very interested in this topic.

"For seven years," I say tiredly. "I met him the day after I got drunk at a high school yacht party and flashed my tits to a group of guys who took pictures. Then I fell off the upper deck and sliced open my back. Wine is my Achilles heel." More so whenever he is involved. "My parents were scandalized. My Dad was terrified I'd be ostracized, and my mother couldn't stop crying at the thought of me being labeled a dirty slut. So, I panicked. The very next day, while bandaged and high on painkillers, I joined a bible study class at my private school, and there I met James Andrew Walker. Jim for short. He told me I was pretty, I told him I was born again, and with my newly reformed attitude, no one could judge me for my hellish lapse in judgment. My parents were happy. I was happy, or at least I thought I was…"

"The marriage was unhappy?"

I nod. Then I shake my head. "Not necessarily at first. We dated for a year before then, but… It was like nothing I did made him happy. How I dressed. How I acted. What I did. Didn't do. I couldn't conceive on *his* timeframe—" I don't go into the details, and luckily he doesn't ask. He just listens, as watchful as ever. "I couldn't have sex the way he wanted. Every day spent with him made me feel like some dirty, disgusting, worthless failure. He was prominent in the church, you see, so I always had to be a 'model wife' for his congregation. Apparently, I failed, because one day, I came to our beautiful home and found him waiting for me with his beautiful secretary whom he'd been sinning with in secret for a year, I think. This, after we were basically separated already so he could 'reevaluate things.' The newer model was pregnant, so divorce city for me. Marital bliss for them."

Saying it all out loud hurts more than I would have anticipated. My eyes burn, and blinking rapidly can't keep one rebellious tear from breaking loose.

"After that, I told myself that I would never, ever beat myself down for anyone else. I would never change who I am to please anyone. If I want to run off on a crazy sexual adventure, then damn it, that's what I'll do."

I look at him, expecting the judgment I'm so used to seeing reflected at me these days. All he does is nod in silent agreement —and in a way, his acceptance is so much worse.

"What happened between you and your brother?" I ask, turning the tables. "You weren't close growing up?"

"You could say that." He's distant again, staring off beyond me. "We weren't close, and for the most part, we grew up apart—he lived with our grandfather after our father's death. Then our uncle…" Disgust colors his voice, making me suspect that he doesn't care very much for that particular family member either. "Even so, we were very much reminded of each other's existence."

"Ah. A sibling rivalry." Lucky for me, I was an only child, but I saw firsthand how nasty sibling battles can go. Uncle Conroy has two sons who constantly vie for his favor. "Let me guess. You were the good twin, and he was the bad?"

"I was the reminder," he says softly. "Of everything he never wanted to be."

"Beautiful, smart, and stubbornly brooding?" I wonder playfully.

He blinks and refocuses on me. His expression is skeptical rather than amused. As if he can't quite understand why I'm trying to joke with him.

"Order something sexy for me in French," I command, spotting our waitress arriving just in the nick of time. "Something sweet."

My heart stops at the devious gleam flashing through his gaze. After scouring the menu for a few more seconds, he turns to our waitress, opens his mouth, and proceeds to utter the most panty-melting stream of words I've ever heard someone speak before. In English or otherwise.

Well, almost. Nothing tops his grunted slip-up from last night, but this comes close.

I smother a groan and try to disguise how my cheeks set on fire by looking down to read my own menu. Once he's finished, I sneak a glance at him through my lashes and hiss in irritation.

He's smugger than ever.

"I've taken the liberty of ordering you a selection of items," he explains, gathering up the menus for the waitress to take. "I will discover which you prefer to dine on the next time you find yourself drunk and hungry while in my bed."

I nearly choke, and I rush to take a sip of water, clearing my throat. "Sorry to break it to you, Vadim, but you won't enjoy having me in a bed with you ever again. Because we aren't having sex again," I feel the need to clarify. "Ever."

He raises an eyebrow, deliciously confused. "You mean to deny yourself of my beautiful cock?"

No fair. I gasp, my brain stalling. When my thoughts come back online, all I can think to utter is, "You're damn right. I'm starting to think that I need to guard myself carefully around you."

Fire flashes through his gaze. "I would never hurt you," he growls —and at the back of my mind, I take comfort in that. Though Jim had said the same thing at one point.

"Not like that," I say softly. "More like… I think you enjoy playing mind games with people, while keeping them at arm's length. Which is fine, I guess. I just don't think I can last on your emotional merry-go-round for long."

Admitting something so honest should feel more alarming than it does. There's just something about him. His face, maybe? I feel so safe when it comes to our conversations. *Which is why you need to run far and fast, girl,* my inner-bitch warns. *Preferably now.*

"Keeping people at arm's length," he murmurs, another amused smile tugging on his mouth. "Usually, I am the one left feeling as though I am on that…merry-go-round as you put it."

"Oh?" I prop my chin on my hand and eye him more closely. His expression remains as neutral as ever, though, on second glance, I notice that his eyes are more hooded than usual. He's recalling his past again. "Your brother?" I guess. "Family? Other businessmen? Frankly, I can't imagine any woman with a functioning libido wanting to keep you at any length, even if you can be a total dick—"

"You asked about my upbringing?" he counters. Something inside me tingles, and I sit forward, suddenly rapt. He was vague about his past before for a reason. The fact that he's bringing it up now makes me feel that something made him change his mind.

"The way my brother and I were raised could be described as a competition," he explains. "Our every waking moment was spent being compared to each other. Who was faster? Stronger? Smarter? Over and over again. Such antics take their toll over time. In many, many ways, I did not measure up to Maxim."

He's so blunt about it, and yet this one fact explains so much about him.

"That's why you hate when I praise you," I say, awed at the realization. "You're so used to being picked apart that your brain can't fathom the concept of a harmless compliment."

"I wouldn't call your words harmless." He shoots me a glance that makes me rush to take another sip of water.

"You mistrust anything that isn't strictly transactional or negative," I add, confident in my psychoanalysis. "The fact that I think you're beautiful, sexy even, with the body of a God makes your brain explode."

"Should an ex-Sunday school teacher speak such blasphemy?" he taunts.

I shrug him off. "Baby, I've decided to no longer be offended by your dickishness. I'm just going to train you as any decent woman would."

His smirk grows, stretching across his pink, tempting mouth. "Train me?"

"Oh, yes!" I clap my hands together at the enormity of the task ahead. "You'll soon come to enjoy my compliments. I think you might even start to crave them, you beautiful man."

"Is that so?" He sits back in his chair and cocks his head to give me a thorough once over. "And these compliments will come without us having sex?"

A challenge, for sure, but one I'm still up for accepting. "Yes," I say with a nod.

"What a shame…" He strokes his finger along his jaw, his gaze reflective. "I was so looking forward to discovering just how you wanted me to use my mouth."

I nearly fall out of my chair. For a horrible second, my thoughts devolve to a frantic mantra of *unfair, unfair, unfair!* When I finally regain my senses, our waitress has returned to set an entire spread of various dishes before us.

Vadim takes the time to name every dish in that drool-worthy accent.

"How did I know you would go for the cream first?" he muses as I grab a fork and shove it into a delicious looking white substance served with jam.

Everything tastes beyond amazing. I sample each dish, circling back to a few in particular, aware of him watching my every move. I've cleared my plate twice when I finally push back from the table in defeat.

"Now what?" I ask as he dabs his mouth with his napkin. Between the two of us, I've eaten seventy-five percent of the meal, but he's barely touched what little items are on his plate. Before I can point out the discrepancy, he shifts his focus to something behind me.

"Now, my business meeting is here." He reaches into his pocket while I glance over my shoulder and spot an older woman wearing a gray suit, her brunette hair pulled back into a severe bun. "What price would you put on having full access to my accounts for the evening?" Vadim questions, his tone suddenly serious.

"H-Huh?" My brain nearly crashes again at the thought of what I could buy if unleashed for several hours. More clothes. More shoes. Maybe I'd take him up on that threat to buy him a new wardrobe? Something tan, or navy, or red. Surprisingly that seems more appealing than the rest.

But then I finally notice the object he has trapped between two fingers and I recoil in alarm. It's a wedding ring. So he wasn't lying about the fake wife.

"Are you insane?"

"Whatever amount you think you could spend, double it," he suggests, but he doesn't extend the ring to me. I have to reach out and take it.

Which I won't. I can't. I…

"Mr. Gorgoshev?" A woman calls from paces away as I finally relent and lunge for the ring. It lands on my palm, and I slip it onto the finger that—until now—had been proudly bare.

Sweat slicks my neck as Vadim stands to greet the woman, and I race to copy him.

"Ms. Anderson, is it?" he says to her warmly. "This is Tiffany, my fiancée."

"P-Pleased to meet you," I stammer while shaking the woman's hand.

She looks different from the typical businesswoman, or even an industry professional for that matter. Her clothing is strictly utilitarian, and the briefcase she carries has seen better days. As she sits, she shuffles through said briefcase and withdraws a stack of documents.

"Ah, yes," she says, furrowing her brow as she reads. "You've applied for permanent residency it looks like. We'll need to do a preliminary house visit, of course, but given the circumstances, I'm sure we can seek placement within a couple weeks. And out of courtesy to you, we can arrange a meeting with the previous family. Your lawyers have assured me that you seek to expedite this case as much as possible?"

"Yes," Vadim nods. In the blink of an eye, his entire posture has shifted. He sits taller, which has the effect of lengthening his body overall and making him seem even more commanding than usual.

Watching him, I quickly lose track of the complicated business terms as they repeatedly discuss placement and a challenging case. Some kind of business he's hoping to acquire? Eventually, the meeting ends as both Vadim and Ms. Anderson stand and shake hands.

"Great. And it looks like you've already secured a property here in the city! If you're okay with everything as specified, then I would love to schedule the first preliminary visit by the end of next week, perhaps?"

"That will suffice," Vadim says, nodding. "I will do everything within my power to ensure that it is perfectly suited."

Smiling, Ms. Anderson walks off. I'm so distracted by watching her departure that I don't notice until it's too late the hand that settles over my lower back.

"A decent performance, *baby*," Vadim murmurs against the column of my throat. "Though next time, try not to drool of utter boredom, *oui*?"

Startled, I swipe at my mouth. Did I?

His laugh reveals that once again, I fell for one of his mind games. Hahaha.

"I should renegotiate my price, adding a deduction for every time you stared off blankly into space, but alas, we have an agreement. Feel free to try your hardest to drive me into bankruptcy. I assure you that you cannot."

"Is that so?" Challenge accepted. My mind reels with the most expensive, exclusive stores I'd never dream of shopping in before. But as Vadim leads me across the lobby to the concierge, I have enough sense to ask. "What was so different about that meeting that you needed a wife present? I'm sure you've made plenty of deals as a bachelor to get where you are."

His jaw twitches—something I'm starting to realize may be his one and only tell. He's hiding something.

"Ms. Connors is to have unlimited use of the town car, this evening," he says to the concierge without addressing my question. "Adieu."

I watch him go, mildly curious. Halfway across the lobby, he pauses and rummages through his jacket pocket.

"I almost forgot this," he calls back to me without turning around. He brandishes a small object between his fingers, forcing me to cross over to him to retrieve it—his credit card. "Spend unwisely," he says, starting off again. "Let's see how much damage you can do."

Challenge accepted. I'm already mulling over what style suit might compliment him the best as I meet my driver out front, and we head toward the shopping district. But at the back of my mind remains this niggling sense that I just missed something.

Something vital.

Something he was willing to bargain unlimited use of his credit card and the promise of a shopping spree to distract me from.

CHAPTER FOURTEEN

I return to the hotel just before midnight in a different vehicle from the sleek, compact model I left in. Halfway through the outing, the poor driver stuck with me had to call for backup and switch out his smaller model for a Range Rover.

Regardless, my purchases are practically spilling out of the SUV. So much so that I have to run to the front desk to request assistance. But the second I give my room number, the hostess raises an eyebrow.

"I'm sorry, Miss," she says. "But it looks like you were checked out at least..." She scrolls through her records. "At least five hours ago. The room has already been cleaned."

"W-What?" Panic grips me so fiercely I have to brace both hands on the counter. *Deep breaths, Tiffy. You still have the bastard's credit card, unless he's already canceled it...*

"Oh! It looks like there was a note left for you. Your husband wanted you to know that he had your things sent home and that he'll be waiting for you there."

"Home?"

She scribbles an address onto a slip of paper. I read it warily, half-expecting to find the listing for the Hotel Six back in California. Instead, I don't recognize the street address or the location.

I try to hand the page back to the hostess. "I think there's some kind of mistake."

"No mistake," she insists. "Our driver will be able to see you home. Thank you so much for your stay, have a wonderful night!"

In a daze, I stagger back out to the car and hand the slip of paper to the driver. Minutes later, we're leaving the city, heading in a direction that seems vaguely familiar. A view of a gleaming body of water pierces a calmer landscape dotted with trees and the average home made of stone or wood. As the driver turns down a long, winding driveway, it clicks.

While this isn't the exact same house his brother Maxim lives in, the one we're pulling up to now looks eerily similar—no doubt within the same location if not the same neighborhood.

It's sprawling, more modern with a winding driveway and acres of neatly manicured property. It's as if someone wanted to copy the coziness of Maxim's home, but applied the crisp, overly neat style of Vadim. The resulting creation is both breathtaking and imposing.

"Allow me to help you with these, Miss," the long-suffering driver insists as he helps me out of the backseat. Between the two of us, we manage to carry most of the packages to the front door, which opens before I can even form a fist to knock.

"Such a late hour," a man suavely remarks. "I was just about to retire to bed and assume you'd used my accounts to charter your own private plane."

"I could do that?" The marvels of men with money. Shaking my head, I try to focus. "What the hell is this, Gorgoshev?" I step forward, barging into the entry, and I drop my packages right there in the middle of an open foyer. While the house may somewhat resemble his brother's from the outside, the inside is all Vadim.

Cool, neutral colors—beige, gray, white, and black. Incomprehensible cleanliness. And then the chaos that comes with me and my five thousand shopping bags.

"Thank you for seeing her home," Vadim warmly tells the driver while tucking a large wad of cash into his palm. "Goodnight."

He heads to the door to see the man off while I take the opportunity to march through the first level of the home. It is massive. A large living room overlooks a view of the water, glistening in the moonlight. Within the same open floor plan is a gorgeous kitchen complete with stainless steel appliances and a double oven.

"Don't tell me you cook as well?" I call over my shoulder, sensing him within earshot.

He chuckles. "No. I had it installed anyway, just in case my fake wife would enjoy the feature. I made sure to cover the cliché basics of what most women supposedly like."

"Wrong." I stick out my thumb and point it to the floor. "I hate cooking."

"Fair enough. It will make for a beautiful focal point during our meals of delivery," he says as I coincidentally pass a sleek bar counter that serves as the bridge to a dining room positioned near a row of massive bay windows. Not far from it is a small lounge complete with black bookshelves already stocked and a neat, official-looking study.

"You really just moved in?" I ask. He makes it look so easy when I can barely organize myself out of a suitcase.

Rather than answer, he trails me until I circle around to the front of the house, my tour completed.

"I suppose you can help me carry these upstairs." I gesture to the mountain of packages. "The brown ones are yours. Any other color is mine."

"The brown ones…" He eyes the mostly brown pile of bags and shoots me a quizzical glance.

"I wasn't sure of your size, so I had to guess," I say, ignoring the implications conveyed by the prospect that I may or may not have spent more time shopping for him than myself. "You can leave mine by the door since I won't be staying here long."

Though should I even consider staying here at all? Spending the night in a fully populated hotel with a dangerously sexy billionaire is one thing. Holing up with him in his private, sprawling mansion is another thing entirely.

But by the time I mount the topmost step of the modern staircase leading upstairs, I promptly forget all about logistics and decency.

"Oh my gosh," I exclaim, spinning in a circle to take in the architecture. High ceilings. Gray, textured walls, and black wooden floors create a sleek, impressive effect so different from my perfect, white-picket-fence dream home. The hall branches into two ends, leading to two separate wings of the house. I start toward the right side, finding a short hallway lined with just two doors. I reach for one, and Vadim makes a sound in his throat that stops me in my tracks.

"That one is private," he says, but his tone makes me bite back a taunting retort. He sounds on-edge for once. Nervous?

A part of me warns that he could be hiding the bodies of his previous fake fiancées in there. Either way, I back off, letting him have this one round.

Turning on my heel, I begin to explore the other wing. The first door I open predictably leads into a massive master suite, but unlike the hotel's more classic décor, this one reads him down to the last detail. Gray walls. Navy accents. A huge bed—far too big for someone intent on living alone.

"Another feature to tempt your fake wife?" I wonder while running my fingers over the navy bedspread.

"No," he says in a deadpan tone. "The closet, however? Well, you be the judge."

An excited thrill has me nearly running to the door he indicates with a curt nod. Sure enough, I find a magical realm of possibility in the form of a closet so big it spans not one, but two entire rooms, each one decked out with plenty of storage for both practical use and display.

He must have it organized into two sections. The first belongs to him, already stocked with a selection of boring, professional attire. The second is mostly bare despite a small collection of neatly arranged Chanel and my previous purchases. What had seemed excessive in the hotel room now looks pitiful, barely taking up a full rack.

"Your future fake wife is a lucky woman," I admit, my heart panging with longing as I spot a full wall of shelves that she could dedicate to purses and shoes alone. Not to mention her ring—for the first time, I inspect the jewelry sparkling on my left hand in full and bite down a groan. The only terms my brain can come up with to describe it are *gorgeous, big ass, diamond.* With difficulty, I turn away and catch him watching me, his devious gaze as unfathomable as ever.

"Chop-chop!" I clap my hands commandingly. "Go fetch my purchases, please. It's time to give you a makeover." I eye him with a raised brow, surprisingly excited to see how he'll look in what I picked out. "We'll cover the basics first," I warn as he strolls into the hall, seemingly unbothered at being bossed around.

"Oh?" he wonders. The subtle, taunting inflection in his tone makes me gulp, but this time I'm prepared with a devious trick to regain the upper hand.

"Undies," I call after him, grinning from ear to ear. "You need a full shakeup from head to toe, baby. Maybe the constriction caused by those horrible boxers is what's making you so mean?"

He laughs, and I sway, knocked off balance. Something tells me that this little plan will backfire.

Spectacularly.

CHAPTER FIFTEEN

In theory, buying him a full range of *tidy-whities* with the intent of having him model them for me sounded fun. Like harmless, mischievous fun while ensuring that I maintain the upper hand in our strange, transactional relationship.

The second he steps from the closet wearing only a pair of black, low riding boxer briefs that, though tight, the salesman at the high-end boutique insisted were more comfortable than going bare, I realize that I've failed.

Game. Set. Match.

"Judging from how your jaw is on the floor, I assume you find these to your liking?" he suspects. Before I can think to stop him, he turns around, displaying his perfectly supported ass, and I can't contain a groan.

"T-Take those off," I spit out, making a mental note to steal every pair of the style I bought and return them. No future fake wife deserves to ever see him in something so sinful.

"Now?" He slips his fingers beneath the waistband, and I practically lunge from the bed and race past him, entering the closet with him on my heels.

"I want you to try on a suit," I decide, spotting a selection he had already partially unpacked. Neatly tucked within a custom garment bag is a rich, brown suit of impeccable quality. Well, almost impeccable. "I had to settle for standard sizing since I don't know your measurements, but they offer custom tailoring, so I took the liberty of including that in the price. Don't have a heart attack when you see the bill."

"I've seen it," he says, coming to stand at my shoulder. I shiver as he reaches around me to finger the sleeve of the suit, testing the quality. "My estimations were on the higher end, but you came close."

I grit my teeth, hating the warmth that spreads through my belly at his nearness. "Was that praise I heard you utter, Mr. Vadim?"

He doesn't answer, and desperate to change the subject, I turn to face him and size him up.

"I'm pretty sure I guessed correctly," I decide, scanning his chest. "Over there are dress shirts."

Obeying my instructions, he promptly unpacks ten shirts in varying colors, ranging from gray to a golden shade of yellow. I made sure to spring for multiple fabrics, including silk and cotton as well. He eyes them all without a word of either agreement or dislike, but his fingers linger over a light blue selection more than the others.

"Blue and brown?" I cock my head and bite my lip in concentration. "An atypical pairing, but let's try it."

He proceeds to dress as I watch him shamelessly from a corner of the closet. When he finally inclines his head for my approval, I think I'm in danger of fainting.

"I need to ban you from wearing blue," I blurt, stunned by how the color animates his features, making his smirk ten times smirkier. "We're done modeling for now." As he takes off the jacket, I re-enter the bedroom, my head spinning. "Where am I going to sleep—"

"I am done modeling," Vadim says, alarmingly stern. "As for you. I insist that you show me at least one of the purchases that rang up to over ten grand at *Atelier Noir*."

I nearly die hearing him mention that number out loud. To a normal person, it's more money than could be feasibly spent on a purchase as frivolous as underwear. But to him, money literally seems meaningless. I don't think it's a front either. He says the numbers with no inflection. Ten dollars or ten grand doesn't mean anything to him either way, and I wonder just how much money he truly has. I'm probably better off not knowing.

"Don't tell me you're ashamed of your selections?" he prods, knowing right where to aim to make me react.

"Fine!" I start toward the doorway, but he clears his throat.

"They're in here." He points to the closet, but I don't have the energy to argue. I'll remove them later.

Sure enough, in the other section of the closet, I find my comparably small arrangement of purchases. My first thought is to try on the more boring, practical bra and panty set I'd gotten. Sometime during my search through the packages, I change my mind and settle on the most daring and risqué.

Jim would die if I ever wore something like this for him—and not in a good way. Die. Come back to life and then restructure his sermons about the dangers of the flesh and how wives are inherently sinful creatures. I chuckle out loud, but it's too close to the truth to be a real joke.

Given Vadim and his damn wall, I picture him eyeing me with no emotion, unmoved by the design either way. So I take my time to ensure I provide him with the full effect.

I strip my Chanel ensemble and hang it. Then I gingerly slip into a sheer emerald green bustier adorned with a dozen hand-sewn ebony roses that decorate the plunging neckline. Admiring myself in the mirror is a surreal experience. I've never felt sexier or more beautiful. A part of me despairs that—for now—this outfit will go woefully unappreciated.

No more sex with Vadim under any circumstances. That doesn't mean I can't needle the hell out of him, though.

"It's a shame we won't be fucking," I declare as I strut into the bedroom, my hips swaying, head thrown back. "Because this little ensemble demands I be…fucked."

Revenge slips from my brain the second I take in his expression. He changed while I'd been in the closet, stripping his suit for that flattering pair of briefs. I must have caught him off guard, in the middle of sitting on the bed. He's frozen mid-crouch, his eyes fixated on my body. A jolt of electricity runs through me as he rakes his gaze up and down the length of me. The poor man doesn't even have the time to rebuild his wall.

I can track every minute reaction transforming his features within the span of a few seconds. A raised eyebrow at my nipples, prominently on display. An appreciative swallow as he roves downward to my practically invisible thong. But then he keeps going down, tracing the curve of my hips and the shape of my thighs, then up to my shoulders and my own throat contracting around a quick swallow.

Our eyes meet, and I realize that I never stopped advancing toward him. In response, he finally moves, lowering himself onto the edge of the mattress as I draw closer. Any second, I expect him to throw his wall back up. Break this spell I can't seem to snap out of as long as he looks at me like…*this.*

With hunger and no ounce of restraint.

My fingers fly up to the neckline of my ensemble, and some reckless impulse makes me finger the thin strap sleeves, pushing his reaction to its limits.

A low hum escapes him as he leans back, taking me in like a man having a world-shattering revelation. One of the *"Holy shit, I'm forever changed"* variety. His eyelids flutter the more I toy with the straps until finally, I let them both slip from my shoulders, sending the neckline plunging.

And he finally moves.

His hands grip my waist first, drawing me into him. Our lips meet next, tongues clashing as my brain goes on hiatus. I wind up straddling him, wantonly rubbing my chest against his, gasping at the friction of the lace over my nipples, enhanced by the heat of his skin. Soon enough, he has the brassiere off and his fingers grope my breasts, kneading them ruthlessly.

"The way you feel…" He trails off, his voice a guttural rumble.

Maybe it's a good thing he doesn't finish that thought? A burst of wetness coats my inner thighs, and I don't think I could survive a second more of him speaking like this.

As if to spite me, his mouth finds my ear as he groans, shifting beneath me so that his legs part, a firm bulge pressing against my mound. "The least I should do is taste you," he murmurs against my flesh. "If we can't fuck."

Total mental shutdown. I'm struck dumb as he lifts me off of him and manipulates me onto my back. All I can do is prop up my upper body on my elbows and watch as he crouches at the foot of the bed between my splayed thighs.

Anticipation builds to a painful degree. As if knowing that, he takes his sweet time trailing his fingers up to my hips and finds the waistband of my thong. One gentle tug and I writhe to assist him.

His lips part as his eyes meet mine. Then he lowers his head and…

I'd imagined what it might feel like to have his mouth on me. Reality takes those fantasies and dashes them. So much for the idea of him partaking in tentative, sensual licking.

He stiffens his tongue, instead plunging it inside me so swiftly I cry out and nearly jolt from the mattress. It's like he's too eager to even play the game he seems to relish in—taunting.

He *takes*. It's a sensation so different from anything else. Silk in lieu of steel, conforming to my every curve and contour. I stiffen as he traces my outer lips, displaying an almost feral attention to every detail. Tasting me in hungry flicks and searing breaths. Panting, I draw my knees up beside him, nonsense spilling from my mouth. Pleas. Praises. Curses.

He is too good at this. Too adept at manipulating his tongue to strike all the right spots. My clit. Then downward, teasing my entrance. Then inside swiftly. Then up again. Such skill betrays that he *had* to have done this before.

But then a growl rips from him, vibrating all the way down to my core. One of shock—like a kid experiencing the taste of candy for the first time. Poof, a glutton is born.

And I'm at his mercy. His hands grip my thighs, nails piercing my flesh in a startling burst of pain. Trapped, I can only squirm as he lunges, applying more pressure. More vigor. More of everything.

My body goes off, climaxing so viciously I barely hear him groan above the sound of my racing heartbeat.

"The taste of you," he grates, sounding crazed. "*Incroyable.* Never get enough…"

And he keeps going, long after I come once. Twice. Again. Soon, I'm shaking, my body drenched in sweat, voice wavering and broken.

"Please. No more… I can't—" Fireworks explode down my spine as he suckles at my clit, drawing out the stimulation to an almost painful degree. "*Vadim!*"

"Addicting woman… I *will* pierce this," he rasps in between nips, and I nearly go off all over again. At the last second, he draws back, leaving me teetering on the edge. Our gazes meet, his unfocused, glimpsed through slits, and I gasp for breath. He looks insane. Mad.

So desirable, it hurts.

"Please." I part my legs eagerly as he steps forward, wrenching his briefs down his hips. His cock juts to attention, so thick my eyelids flutter at the sight.

He doesn't hesitate to mount me, shoving in so deep I come again. And again.

Lost in a haze of pleasure, I hear him curse, his hips slamming over mine. Like gasoline poured onto a roaring inferno, the sensation of his release flooding my sheath sets me off yet again.

I cling to him, clawing at his back, marking him as brutally as he fucks his pleasure into me, still moving until his cock finally softens.

Spent and breathless, the reality doesn't kick in until I'm staring up at the ceiling, aware of him partially on top of me, his mouth on my throat.

So much for no sex.

CHAPTER SIXTEEN

I am so royally fucked. Literally and figuratively.

I wake up beside Vadim again—this time with one hand on my ass and the other on my tit. I lie facing him, his arm around my hips, his body relaxed, his face utter perfection. My heart pangs as I blink my eyes open to see him, bathed in the glow of early dawn.

I drink him in, barely able to keep from touching him. My brain is still drunk off the sex, and dangerous thoughts creep in. Like how good it feels lying beside him. His posture alone conveys that he feels the same way, relishing our carnal attraction. Lust isn't an affliction he's forced to suffer. If anything, he has to surrender to it.

But how long can I stomach this before I get hopelessly addicted?

It's like he's always reading my mind, even while unconscious. He stirs, his eyes opening, as a part of me warns that it's already too late. Those dark irises take me in leisurely, still unfocused from sleep. A groan rips from him as his tongue traces a path along his lower lip.

"You are so beautiful."

And he means it. He truly thinks I'm beautiful enough that he slips up and breaks his most stubborn social rule. A frown shapes his mouth as he realizes what he's done, and he rolls onto his back. Both of his hands withdraw from me, and I can practically see him rearranging the bricks of his invisible wall.

"Don't be mean to me." I shuffle forward and mold myself against him. The logical part of my brain is screaming, but I don't care. Rejection is a pill I can't swallow right now. Not when I can still feel him inside me, and my brain is still churned to mush. Jim always pushed me away.

Vadim sighs but relents to the contact. Reluctantly, his arm slips beneath my waist again, and I wiggle into his touch, overwhelmed with relief. A pity cuddle is beyond his comfort level—I know that. But he endures this one anyway. Later, I'll go over the repercussions.

Now?

I'm dizzy, and clinging to him seems to be the only way I can ground myself.

"I loved having you go down on me," I confess against his ear. His jaw twitches, but the depth of his expression is hard to make out from this angle. Good? Bad? "I love how you felt," I continue, letting my eyes drift shut as his heat thrums through me, more relaxing than the world's best wine. "I love when you lose control. I love when you fuck me wild—"

"Enough to stay?"

"Hmm?" I peel one eye open only to find him staring at me intently, all traces of lust erased. He's serious.

"Enough to let me pierce you?" He slides his hand along my thigh, raising goosebumps.

I sink against him again and let out a dreamy sigh. "Enough to consider letting a trained professional pierce me, yes." I may even mean it. Just thinking about how a piercing might have enhanced my pleasure last night?

I'm beyond tempted.

That seems to placate him enough that he relaxes beside me. We must drift off like this. When I come to again, I'm lying naked with the sheets kicked down to my ankles and the space beside me glaringly empty. Confused, I roll over to catch a half-naked Vadim strolling across the room, wearing only a towel slung over his waist. Dripping water, his curls hang freely, and I have to clamp my knees together as I take him in.

"You showered without me." I sound devastated by the fact.

Frowning, he doesn't seem to realize why.

I flip onto my back, but I don't bother to cover myself with a sheet. "Letting me suck you off in the shower should have been your number one priority after last night," I point out. "Fair is fair."

He chuckles, strolling toward the closet with renewed confidence. "The things you say…"

"Are you leaving?" I sit up and finally reach for the end of the comforter, drawing it around me. A row of floor-to-ceiling windows provides a bird's eye view of the surrounding landscape.

It looks to be early in the afternoon, though cloud cover and a light rainfall make it harder to pinpoint a time for sure.

"I have some errands to run," he admits. Then almost hesitantly, he adds, "You are welcome to join me."

"Really?" I bound from the mattress before he can change his mind.

"The bathroom is through that door," he says, nodding toward a polished, silver one in the corner of the room. I step through it only to enter a dream world formed of stainless-steel fixtures with the main attraction being a clawfoot tub positioned near a view of the water.

It's also infuriatingly modern.

If the shower at the hotel confounded me, this one leaves me hopelessly confused as to where to begin—it's a panel built into the wall in the center of a huge stall enclosed by glass. In the end, I give up and call for help.

An amused Vadim appears at my shoulder seconds later, dressed in the brown suit and blue shirt ensemble he modeled for me last night. His breath tickles my shoulder as he explains how to operate the shower. Once I have the water pressure set to my liking, I lather up, only to realize that—rather than leave the bathroom—he's seated leaning against a row of marble-topped counters, watching me bathe.

A sly smile tugs on my mouth. I feel like some concubine at the mercy of her captor—and I abuse his attention to the fullest. Closing my eyes, I toss my head into the spray and shamelessly stroke myself with a washcloth. Up and down. Between my legs. I pay special attention to my breasts and the curve of my ass, turning around as I do so that my back faces my audience.

Even above the relentless roar of the water, I still hear his groan.

When I finally finish, however, and step from the shower, he's gone. I have to pad across the room and grab my own towel from a silver rack. Before any real disappointment can set in, he reappears, a strip of fabric slung across his arm.

"I can't risk you spending hours to dress yourself today," he says by way of explanation. He unfurls the fabric, revealing one of my new dresses.

"Do you think green is my color?" I ask, eyeing the selection skeptically. It's an eye-catching A-line day dress with a modest neckline and black buttons rimmed in gold going down the front. I may have picked it out to wear on my own, but the color is suspiciously close to that of the lingerie I wore last night.

Sporting a smirk, I drop my towel and pull the dress on. Ever the smart ass, he also supplied me with a pair of lace panties it seems —but no bra.

"How scandalous, Mr. Gorgoshev," I scold as I prance past him into the bedroom, and my nipples promptly harden at the shift in temperature.

I can't help feeling like the joke is on me, though, as he follows behind and swears under his breath. "*Merde.*"

Apparently, this dress hugs my ass in a way he appreciates.

Tit for tat.

Downstairs, he fishes a pitcher of orange juice from the fridge and proceeds to pour two glasses. On the counter, someone already laid out a cold spread of delicate glass bottles of jam, a bowl of fresh fruit, and a basket containing an assortment of bread from croissants to a baguette.

"Did you leave these out all night?" I wonder, shooting him a curious glance.

"No," he says while handing me a glass of juice. "Ena did. He doubles as both my security and my chef when the urge strikes him. He makes himself scarce, and I specifically requested he stay out of sight to avoid startling you. The presence of security can sometimes make those around me uneasy."

"Ah." Given how much money he likes to throw around, a highly trained security team makes sense. Is it creepy that some stranger had access to the property without me knowing? A little. "I'm guessing that Ena was responsible for delivering my Chanel the other day?"

He nods and picks through the breadbasket, settling on a piece of the baguette. "As I mentioned, I told him to make himself scarce, but sometimes he gets persistent when he believes I'm not eating enough."

"Because of your diabetes," I deduce softly. Reaching out, I playfully tug on his sleeve, surprised when his mouth twitches into a fleeting smile. "Don't tell me you're one of those workaholic men who recklessly disregard their health in their pursuit of the almighty dollar."

"Not quite." He trails his fingers across the lid of a light-yellow jam as if mulling over whether or not to divulge more about himself than he already has. "Sometimes, I may go days without eating if I am not reminded. It's not a conscious choice, mind you."

"Oh?" I watch him, my throat thickening. Could he suffer from an eating disorder?

"When I was a child… Meals did not come regularly." He deftly opens the jam bottle and slathers a healthy amount onto his bread slice. "I learned to suppress my hunger to escape the torment. And with insulin in short supply, doing so probably saved my life in the long run. Even in my adulthood, I've found that it's been difficult for me to revert from that mindset."

Building horror tempers my curiosity to ask him more. I don't like how he looks whenever he recalls his past. He isn't reminiscing over wonderful Christmases and holidays spent on his uncle's vineyard, that's for sure.

Guilt stings as I regret ever needling him at all. To lighten the mood, I snatch a croissant and proceed to shove half of it into my mouth.

He eyes me quizzically, his upper lip quirking, and boom. He's distracted.

"Try not to choke," he warns, dabbing at the corner of my mouth with a crisp white napkin. "I may have use for this throat yet." He grazes the quivering column with his thumb, and my brain threatens to go offline again.

"The things you say," I scold once I manage to swallow.

He laughs and gathers up the assorted breakfast items, carrying them to the glass dining table. The mysterious Ena must have been the one to set the table for two, as well as put a neat stack of newspapers near the place setting Vadim claims for himself.

"Is this how you impress your other women?" I taunt as he lifts the topmost paper from the stack and proceeds to flip through it. "Proving yourself to be a worldly and knowledgeable businessman?"

He doesn't look up from his task, but his mouth quirks. Another smile? "I prefer to brush up on the current events every morning. It is my routine."

"Ah." I stuff my face with another bite of bread and settle in to watch him. He skims through the major sections of the paper, paying attention to the world news and politics before heading to the business section. As he reads, his expression shifts from thoughtful, to concerned, to neutral again. When he finally thrums through the last stack, he looks up as if surprised to find me still here.

"You aren't bored?"

"No," I admit truthfully. It shouldn't be this damn enthralling just ogling someone as they go about their simple routine.

His smirk returns, and he downs the rest of his orange juice before standing.

We cut through the back of the house, passing through a doorway that opens into a spacious garage containing three vehicles in varying degrees of flashy. The most conservative is a black van. Then a gray compact car, and then finally the cherry red sports car he drove to his brother's house. In some ways, they remind me of three distinct personalities. The surly, mysterious Vadim, the cold Vadim, and the warm, slightly unpredictable daredevil who spanks women in one moment and manipulates them the next.

"After you." He ushers me into the passenger's seat, and within minutes we're heading toward the city.

Our first destination is a tall, sleek office building in the heart of a mass of skyscrapers clawing at the sky. A simple logo adorns the front façade—three emerald-colored circles interlinked beside a crisp font read *Eingel Health Industries*.

"Is this your company?" I ask as he parks in a reserved space at the heart of a parking garage at the base of the building.

"One of them," he says. "I no longer have a role in the day-to-day operations, but my share of the stock allows me to utilize an office in the American headquarters whenever I'm in town."

"A hotel room in California. An office here in Fair Haven. It seems as though you bounce from city to city, Vadim." Though the woman from his meeting yesterday did mention that he only recently bought his house.

"I've yet to find anything worth keeping me in one place for too long," he admits while we enter a polished lobby and take an elevator to the top floor. As if in afterthought, he adds, "Anything that requires me, anyway."

And yet, all of a sudden, it seems, he's gotten the urge to buy a fake wife and purchase a sprawling mansion near his estranged brother? I contemplate asking him as much, but I can almost see the invisible bricks of his wall threatening to fall into place the second I push him too far.

So I bite my tongue and follow him down what appears to be an executive suite guarded by a single secretary seated behind a desk. She eyes Vadim and then does a swift doubletake, nearly falling off of her chair.

"M-Mr. Gorgoshev! We weren't expecting you. It's been so long since your last visit—"

"Over a year, I think," Vadim says with a charming grin. Jealousy prickles through my belly, though when I scan his expression, it's the neutral detachedness I've come to expect from him.

"Yes, a year," the secretary says solemnly. "Your office is just as you left it. I'll have fresh coffee sent in immediately."

"For two," Vadim adds before taking my hand. I warily follow him past the secretary and into a spacious office that looks fit for a CEO—not a "casual investor" who hasn't bothered to visit this place in over a year.

"Were you on an extended vacation?" I ask him playfully as he claims a leather armchair placed before a polished wooden desk while I collapse into a matching seat before him.

"Something like that." He looks away. *Thunk.* Before I know it, the wall has come down between us. I'm surprisingly stung—more than I should be. Cracking him takes so much effort. I'm not used to being the aggressive party in any relationship.

Not that this is a relationship.

Still. I can't resist testing one of his invisible bricks for any hint of weakness.

"How long were you in Cali for?"

He frowns, stroking his chin. "A month? Two months? The days tend to blur together. I was here not too long ago, but that trip was not for business."

Ah. I nod. "So, what made you want to come back now?"

Especially after a year of absence.

His smile turns cold. "One could say…complications within my family. But I'm here for good. At least if…"

"If?" I prod, leaning forward. We're in a tug of war, I sense—fighting over the position of one of his bricks. I'm pushing hard, but he's fighting just as relentlessly to keep it in place. With a sigh, he sits back, and something gives.

I win this round.

"There is something I want," he says carefully—deliberately vague, but it's a start, so I bite my tongue. After a few tense seconds, he rewards me by speaking some more. "Something I want enough to fight for, even if it means staying in this God-forsaken place. I won't let anyone stop me. This time, Maxim won't drive me off."

A stupid, careless part of me wants to suspect that he means a relationship. A relationship he might have spontaneously discovered with a certain redhead. But that's not it. His expression radiates emotion for once—a raw, feral energy that makes me shudder. Whatever his goal is, it requires him to fake a wife and risk living within his brother's volatile orbit to attain it.

And maybe I'm a teensy bit jealous.

"Can I have a hint?" I ask sweetly.

He blinks and looks up as if remembering I'm even here. Then he casually tugs open a drawer on his end and fishes out a silver pen. "I need to work."

His tasks this time stretch well into the early afternoon. Again, I think I should be bored, forced to watch him, left with no other entertainment. But damn, even watching this man pour over reports and make phone calls is riveting. It's almost like observing a ballet dancer gracefully in his element—a master at work.

Eventually, he puts his papers away and seems to take pity on me because he stands and extends his hand to help me to my feet as well.

"Lunch," he explains, leading me out into the hall. I expect him to take me back to the car, but instead, he turns into a large boardroom set with a spread fit for a king. "I took the liberty of having a few things delivered," he explains while guiding me to a seat near the head of the table while he takes the one across from me.

"I think I recognize that brand of wine," I say cynically, eyeing the infamous bottle of vintage that had been my kryptonite back at the hotel suite. "Are you trying to ply me, Mr. Vadim?"

"Yes." He sits back further, threading his fingers together. A part of me quivers, recognizing that I'm on an unfair playing field. This room, this location is an arena best suited to give him the advantage.

So, like any sore loser, I play dirty. I yawn as if bored and reach up to flick open the topmost button of my dress. Then another. Another. The barest tease of cleavage is enough to dampen his smug grin to acceptable levels. All is fair in war, after all.

"There is something I want to discuss," he says, cutting to the chase.

"Yes?"

"You teased me about being pierced before," he begins, laying one of the most dangerous topics on the table. "Were you serious?"

"Yes," I blurt automatically. A sexy piercing would be the introduction to the kink I've been fantasizing about. My relationship with him aside, why should I let a harmless fling stop me? Especially if he's planning on paying for it.

"But," I add, still eyeing the table. "I want to renegotiate my previous price—"

"Anything." The heat in his voice draws my attention, and I sorely regret facing him directly. I got my wish. His wall came down, but I'm no match for what I find lurking beneath it. Dark eyes heavy-lidded and focused, a jaw clenched to brooding perfection and pink lips slightly moistened by a slithering tongue. There's no way to describe the reaction other than raw, naked lust.

"You really want me to do this," I whisper hoarsely. Should I be horrified? I'm not. I'm freaking thrilled. My mind skips ahead, imagining him, teasing some delicate silver piercing with his teeth. Even the thought makes synapses in my brain explode and fire at random.

"Yes," he confesses without shame. "I... I would love to pierce you."

Holy hell. I have to keep from fanning myself, and all I can think to blurt out is, "Why?"

He sits back, eyeing me objectively. His gaze flickers down my torso, settling where the table obscures. "I am intrigued... No. I *love*—" his tongue fumbles with the word, betraying how little he must say it. If ever. A part of me feels oddly pleased that few women probably ever hear him utter it in this husky, dangerous tone. Overall, I'm more alarmed than ever. "I love the idea of you entrusting yourself to me."

Heat pools beneath my legs so hotly my brain has trouble catching up. But when it does, I blink, snapping from the daze as something clicks.

"You mean, *you* actually want to pierce me?"

He raises an eyebrow as if the concept isn't totally insane. "I would prefer to be the only one to pierce you."

I shake my head. "Sorry, but I can't just let anyone put holes into my nether regions." There are some lines even I'm not willing to cross. "Anyone but a trained professional."

His mouth quirks into an expression of utter sin. "Luckily for us both, I am a trained professional."

I scoff. "Really? For real, or did you just learn by watching videos online or something?"

His murky gaze offers no insight, and I feel stunned, more off-balance than ever.

"Let me guess," I spit in exasperation, "you pierced yourself?"

His smile falls flat, betraying a hint of vulnerability, and my eyes go so wide I'm sure they'll pop right out of my head.

"You did? You pierced yourself!" I scramble upright and circle the table until I reach his chair.

"There are cameras," he warns in that unnervingly neutral tone. But I don't care. I straddle him anyway, forcing him to push back from the table to give me enough room. If there are cameras, I figure my hunched frame shields how my hand slithers between us, finding the front of his slacks.

He watches on in cautious amusement as I tug open his fly and slide my hand beneath the fabric, cupping his shaft. Surprise, surprise, he's hard, pulsing against my palm. But foreplay isn't on my mind as I drag my thumb across the crown, gently—very, very gently—probing one of the protruding silver beads capping the bar of his piercing.

"Why on earth would you pierce yourself?" I croak, still stroking him. But he already gave me the answer, didn't he? For control. To exert ownership over himself that no one else could. Why might he be driven to such an extreme? I shouldn't want to know.

"I may or may not have been in my right mind," he confesses, his eyes narrowing further with every hesitant brush of my thumb. Maybe I should stop touching him like this? I can't seem to.

"*You*, on the other hand, I will treat with the utmost care," he promises, his voice thickening, making my tongue moisten. Damn, he makes being stabbed through with a needle sound… irresistible. "I will even numb you first so that you feel no pain."

"No pain… You pierced yourself *raw?*" I blurt, my voice so loud anyone passing by could hear me. "Baby!" I cup his jaw with my free hand, forcing him to meet my gaze. He stares back blankly, as if he can't quite decide why I care. Deep down, I don't know why either, but the thought of him hurting himself—because that's the only way to describe it—makes me…

Ache in ways I never have.

"Tell me why," I whisper, running my lips over his jaw, sensing it stiffen. Then soften. "I'll let you put as many holes in me as you want, *just tell me why.*"

"My feelings have changed over time," he says carefully, his gaze growing distant. "But I would be lying if I claimed that my original goal was anything other than…mutilation."

My heart lurches at the thought of it. Someone so lost, so tormented that driving a needle through his own penis was the only way he could regain control. Over his body. Over himself.

Voice rasping, I murmur, "Why?"

"I thought it would make me unappealing," he confesses tonelessly. "Grotesque. That no one could derive pleasure from it. No one would ever crave it—me—honestly. I could track their intentions then. Anyone who claimed otherwise, obviously had ulterior motives. I would be on guard."

Such a freaking man. So paranoid, he would turn his own penis into a lie detector. A faulty one at that.

Overwhelmed, I release him and twist around until I face the world looming beyond a row of full-length windows. The city stares back, cold and lifeless. Why he would choose to settle here, of all places? I can't imagine.

Or maybe that's the point? Denying himself of beauty and pleasure is starting to seem like his defining trait.

"*That's* why you rejected me after the first time we had sex," I deduce out loud. "I called your cock beautiful."

"A lie, of course," he admits, his breath hot against my ear. "Or so I thought at the time."

"And now?" I crane my head back, my chest tightening at how tormented he can seem in one brief moment—and then hard the next.

"I may be warming up to the idea that you have a very warped sense of attraction."

Ass. I hiss in annoyance, but I find myself leaning into him, bracing my back against his chest, allowing his mouth the nuzzle the crook of my shoulder.

"Is that why you want to pierce me?" I wonder, almost fearing what he might say in response. "To mutilate me—"

"Never." A growl rips from his throat, vibrating with indignation. One of his hands lands over my thigh, radiating a power that makes me feel deliciously small. At his mercy. "On you? Such adornment could *only* be beautiful."

He treats that word so reverently, laving it with his tongue, making me wish he would say it over and over again. Or not. His cock is pulsing against my ass, spurring an answering wetness to coat my inner thighs. Cameras or not, I can't resist rocking against his hardness, teasing a groan from him.

"Do I have your answer?" he grates through clenched teeth.

I only need to think for a second before I'm nodding. "Yes. You can pierce me. I… I *want* you to pierce me. But when?"

He grips my hips and gently lifts me from his lap, chuckling in a low, lethal tone. "I will pick a time most agreeable to me. I don't think I'll tell you, though. Not until I'm good and ready."

"Ass!" I manage to stand on trembling legs, and he rises as well, smoothing his hands over my hips to help right my balance.

"Yes," he murmurs while sliding his palm down to the back of my thigh. "Ass. You have a lovely one, I must say."

My face heats, my thoughts threatening to boil once more. "Is that a compliment, Mr. Vadim?"

He doesn't answer. His hand reluctantly leaves my ass only to capture my wrist, steering me after him down the hall and back into the office. He heads past the desk, opening a door that leads to an executive bathroom, complete with its own marble fixtures and walk-in shower.

"Impressive," I mutter as he guides me back against a row of counters placed before a pristine mirror. He spins me to face him, and I suck in a breath at what I find when I meet his gaze.

Fire.

The brooding businessman has dropped his wall again. Heat sears through my belly, enhancing the moisture already trapped by the fabric of my lace panties. I arch my back, clamping my knees together.

A twitch in his jaw reveals that he's well aware of my actions.

"I do believe there is some policy on the books that cautions against the CEO or whatever you are trapping innocent young ladies within bathrooms—"

His lips settle over mine firmly—and yet hesitant. As if he's testing out what a kiss might feel like in this context. If I had an ounce of self-control, I'd remain still and let him explore in peace. But I don't.

My fingers sink through his hair, pulling him into me as I adjust my hips, teasing the front of his pants until he's panting, his eyes unfocused. He reaches out, snatching my wrist, and guides my fingers to his still open fly. I don't think he even realizes what he's doing.

I cup him fully and sink to my knees, relishing how he groans, his hands settling over my scalp.

"I would like to make an addendum to our previous arrangement regarding the piercing," I hum, letting my breath wash over him. His piercing jumps, his body rigid.

"Anything," he rasps in that beautiful, enticing way.

I extend my tongue, tapping his thickening crown. "I want to know everything about you," I confess, lapping at a bead of fluid that weeps from him. My core clenches, my breaths thinning. Despite my faked confidence, I'm rapidly in danger of a total factory shutdown where my brain is concerned. For some reason, this matters, though. Saying this out loud, knowing he can hear me. "Everything. The good stuff. The bad stuff—" I capture the topmost silver bead between my thumb and flick it gently. He rocks on his heels, hissing something I don't understand. French? "I want to know about your past. What you do for fun. Everything." I take him into my mouth, swirling my tongue around the pulsing head of him.

A grunt revs in his throat as his nails tease my scalp. Could the icy businessman be losing control? Gosh, I hope so.

I bob my head and suck harder to encourage him. His piercing feels electric every time my tongue strikes it, his vibrating moans intoxicating. I'd always been intrigued by fellatio, but I never knew giving it could feel so...

Empowering.

I have him in the palm of my hands—literally. His balls swell, his body quaking, and his grip becomes insistent.

"Not...in your mouth," he grates.

But I can't resist. Like a child with a treat, I devour him with vigor. Deepthroating him isn't in the realm of possibility now, but I take him as far as I can, giving him a taste of what it could be like. What *we* could be like.

Fire. Sizzling, crackling, pulsating energy.

My throat is already contracting the second the first taste of him floods my mouth, and this time I drink him all the way down.

Panting, he slumps against the counter, comfortably crushing me between it and his muscular thighs. Pleased with myself, I rear back to watch his face as he stares down on me, his eyes wide. He's having another world-altering revelation, I suspect. Still breathing heavily, he reaches down and strokes my bottom lip, chasing a stray bit of moisture.

"Insolent witch," he rasps hoarsely. "I didn't want to risk… Should I punish you for disobeying?"

I nod, a part of me way too eager to take him up on that threat.

But he stands upright with an urgency that displaces some of the lust. He adjusts his pants and helps me to my feet. With a wet paper towel, he cleans me up, and we escape the bathroom together, then the office entirely.

Minutes later, we're back in the car. He drives with one hand while the other finds mine, capturing it. I marvel at the sight of our combined fingers, my heart racing.

"More work?" I wonder, as he lazily merges into traffic.

He shakes his head. "I'm done for the day. I'm thinking of heading home." His eyes flicker toward mine, and for once, I know exactly what he's thinking. Dirty man.

I can't deny the idea of crawling onto him the second we enter his house is very tempting. I'm still on edge, and at the back of my mind, I realize that I never actually came in the bathroom. I didn't even notice. Somehow, watching him had been more than enough to satisfy me in the moment. And now, I crave something…more.

A taste of him more intimate than even his literal taste.

"I want you to take me somewhere," I tell him, flipping our clasped hands so that I stroke the veined back of his. "Somewhere special to you. I wasn't kidding before."

And maybe that should scare me. The more I learn of Vadim Gorgoshev, the more I forget my internal promise. This is all just fun and games. Nothing serious. I'm not falling for him after barely a week.

I'm not.

"You really want to know?" he wonders, his voice suddenly cold, devoid of heat. I stiffen, alarmed, and sit straighter in my seat. "Then I'm afraid there is something I haven't told you about. Someone."

I choke down a panicked swallow. Someone? A real wife he has hidden in a storage shed somewhere?

"Who?"

He sighs, and casually manipulates the steering wheel, leaving the main street altogether. "The love of my life," he says simply. "It's time you've met her."

CHAPTER SEVENTEEN

I want to vomit until he parks before a building on the outskirts of the city—presumably the home of his supposed true love. As soon as we exit the car and I inhale a familiar, musky scent, some of my panic eases, replaced by grim amusement.

"Don't tell me your true love lives in a barn?" I ask as he leads me into a wide, spacious stable overlooking a vast expanse of green pasture.

"Oh yes," he says with a stern nod. "This is her kingdom, and here is the queen..."

I gasp as he leads me to a stall where the most beautiful white mare I've ever seen immediately sticks her head over the low door. She whinnies in greeting, her eyes gleaming at the sight of Vadim. True love in its purest form.

A love that seems wholly reciprocated.

"And here she is," he gushes, stroking her ivory mane. "My Zzazza. My sweet." He brushes his lips along her cheek. "The only girl to ever claim my heart."

"Should I be jealous?" I wonder as I creep forward and offer my hand for her to sniff. Money must not really be an option for him. She's gorgeous, and her "kingdom" appears to be a massive stable housing only her and two other horses, each within their own spacious stall.

"Who is this?" I ask, spotting a darker, chestnut face eyeing me from another stall.

"Donali," he explains, reluctantly leaving Zzazza. "And that handsome gelding is Markesh. All beautiful. All who own a piece of my soul."

"You own this entire stable?" I ask incredulously.

A sly smile shapes his mouth, and his eyes gleam in a way I've never seen, resonating warmth. "I rent it out to a few students who give Donali and Markesh all the love they could ever need. But my girl Zzazza? She is all mine." He returns to the mare, rubbing her affectionately. "But I have sorely neglected her. For that, I apologize, my sweet."

"Don't tell me you haven't seen her in a year?" I move to stand by his side, watching as he showers the horse with murmured praises and generous petting.

Something that could be guilt darkens his gaze as he withdraws from her with a sigh. "Ena has been keeping you company in my absence, hmm?" She knickers as if in agreement. "I told the old bastard to take you out at least once a day."

"She must be a dream to ride," I say.

A small smile shapes his mouth. "That she is. It's been far too long since we've taken a nice long one, hasn't it?"

Something about how he tailors his voice for the horse alone makes my chest feel tight. Awe? Maybe more jealousy too.

"We could now?" I suggest, only to realize that a dress worth several thousand grand and a tailored suit probably aren't the best items of clothing to wear horseback riding.

Vadim scoffs. "Most women would be horrified at the prospect of smelling like an animal and risk breaking a sweat." His eyes glitter playfully, and I puff myself up, placing my hands on my hips.

Challenge accepted.

"Is that so? My mother bred thoroughbreds for fun when she wasn't playing the socialite housewife. You should be worried if your riding skills will even impress me. If I had suitable clothing, I'd have you take me out in a heartbeat. We could always ride naked," I add, savoring the faint color that paints his cheeks even as his expression remains stubbornly neutral. "But that might offend your workers' sensibilities."

"Luckily for you, I keep a spare set of jodhpurs here," he says, leaning in close, his breath hot on my neck. "And I am more than willing to display my skills for your judgment."

I crane my neck back and meet his gaze with a lazy smile. "You're on."

HE IS AN AMAZING RIDER. Balanced in front of him, I can sense every slight shift in his posture as he guides the horse beneath us down a winding path through a vast range of fields. He and Zzazza move so beautifully in sync it's as if they're reading each other's minds.

And maybe I'm more than a *little* jealous now.

I had wanted him to *tell* me more about himself, but I'm starting to realize that this way is so much better. Seeing it for myself. Feeling the air whip through my hair as a powerful, massive creature moves beneath me primarily of its own will. It's an illusion of control built mostly on trust, and I think I understand a fraction of his obvious passion for it. And once again, my impression of him is turned on its head.

We return to the stables far too soon and change into our regular clothing. Night is just starting to darken the horizon by the time we approach the house.

"You head in," Vadim says as he pulls into the garage. "I have some things to attend to. I'll be back soon."

His hand lingers over mine as I reluctantly leave the car, holding me until the last possible second.

"Where are you going?" I ask, suspicious.

He laughs. Such a sinful sound. "I think you enjoy it more when you can't anticipate my actions," he says smugly. "I'll be back soon."

He drives off, and I watch him go with a frown. The man is starting to know me too damn well. Enough for me to admit that he's right—I enjoy the thrill of his mystery now more than ever.

Sighing, I enter the house, relieved to find the door unlocked. I can't help but pout as I wander the spacious interior all alone. I could have begged him to take me, but even I can take a hint. He wanted to be alone.

Probably to head to some hotel bar and troll for another fake wife.

Knock it off, Tiffy, warns my inner bitch. *You're getting too involved with him. If anyone should be leaving, it's you.*

I should. I even linger near the staircase, toying with the idea of running upstairs, packing a few things, and then escaping into the dead of night with only a note left for him on a pillow or something equally as dramatic.

Instead, I keep moving, heading for the kitchen in a frantic search for wine. I round the bar counter and promptly scream as my eyes fall over a figure rummaging through the fridge.

He's bulky, dressed in a scarred black leather jacket and jeans. A blunt mop of dark hair frames an angular, round face set with almond-shaped brown eyes. The man's tan skin enhances their color to a piercing degree as he inclines his head to observe me. Unimpressed, he returns his attention to the fridge.

Assuming a thief would show more discretion in front of a potential witness, I try to think of another explanation for his appearance. Then I remember. "Are you Ena?" I ask as the man turns, closing the fridge door with his hip. In his arms is an array of more fresh fruit that he arranges onto the counter. My heart stutters as he snatches a knife from a nearby drawer and promptly halves an apple.

"You," he says, his voice gruff and heavily accented with a dialect I can't place. "Mr. Vadim eat—" He points to the fruit before lifting an orange and cutting it into slices. "Yes?"

"Y-Yes," I croak, warily inching toward a stool. "You want us to eat—"

"No. No." He faces me fully, his eyes narrowed. "You *make* him eat—" Again, he points to the food. "Or his brain goes." He adjusts his thumb and forefinger into a terrifying imitation of a gun. Then he presses the tip of it to his temple and mimes pulling the trigger. "You make him eat. Yes?"

"Yes," I insist, my voice rasping.

"Good." He marches to a nearby cupboard, surprisingly light on his feet despite his girth, which isn't entirely composed of muscle. His build reminds me of a Sumo wrestler, and I realize why Vadim might use him as a bodyguard.

He opens a cupboard and withdraws a wooden bowl. As he neatly arranges the fruit inside it, I contemplate how rude it might seem if I escape upstairs. Not out of fear—mainly to hide. There's a tension in his body that unsettles me in a way I can't explain. I doubt he'd hurt me, but I get the sense that I am sorely not welcome here.

And not just in this house, but Vadim's orbit in general.

"You go to brother dinner?" Ena grunts the second I start to shimmy in the direction of the hall.

"Um…yes," I stammer. "With um, I think his name is Maxim and—"

"He should not go." He slams his knife onto the counter and storms to the sink to wash his hands. "Brother makes Mr. Vadim go crazy," he adds once he shuts off the water. "He goes for you."

I blink. "I'm sorry?"

Hissing in disgust, Ena whirls to face me, and there's no mistaking the raw anger lashing toward me like a whip. "You are toy in brothers' game—" He jabs a finger in my direction. At the back of my mind, I register that he only has three remaining on his right hand. "You go. He stays. So go." He points in the direction of the front door.

I'm too stunned to say anything. By the time I regain control over my mouth, Ena is already stomping through the kitchen, heading toward the exit himself. "You bad for Mr. Vadim," he says coldly. "You go. He better."

A second later, the front door slams behind him.

Overwhelmed, I reclaim my stool and bury my face in my hands. Maybe the disgruntled bodyguard is right? Playing this game with Vadim—no matter how fun it might be in the interim—is only going to end badly. His idea of a relationship seems to extend about as far as his credit card limit and as for me...

I'm not looking for anything serious. Because doing so would be a total betrayal to my new, improved independence freshly reclaimed after years stuck in my marriage with Jim. After nearly a decade, what do I have to show for it? A trail of broken dreams, wasted potential, and no survival skills to speak of, other than living off a mixture of my trust fund and alimony.

Jumping into another relationship—real or otherwise—could only be deemed as unhealthy at best. Pathetic at worst.

It's not like I'm falling for him, the beautiful, sexy, billionaire of unknown wealth who delivers the best sex I've had to date. That would be recklessly irresponsible. So it's a good thing I'm not thinking about him right now, wondering what the hell he's getting up to without me.

I'm not.

To distract myself, I mentally catalog all my potential outfit pairings utilizing my new wardrobe. I don't even notice that someone is behind me until it's too late. They touch my shoulder, and I nearly jump out of my skin.

"I didn't mean to startle you," a voice like sin drips into my ear. The owner's trademark smugness proves that yes, startling me was exactly his intention.

My eyes narrowing, I whip my head around, startled by his charming grin. That ride did wonders for him. His eyes gleam, and his posture seems relaxed for once. Even his smile looks more natural and less like a mask anchoring his wall.

I'm instantly on guard.

I sniff the air and find myself scanning him for any hint of lipstick or perfume—any trace of another woman. Because I'm an insane, irrational cow who has no right to be jealous. When I finally notice the object balanced on his palm, I wrinkle my nose in suspicion.

"What is that?"

A box, it seems. Light blue, wrapped with a white ribbon that makes it suspiciously resemble a present.

His grin widens. Then he notices something on the glass dining table and crosses to it, setting the small box aside. "Good. I've been waiting for this to arrive."

So his henchman's visit wasn't all about food, I realize. Ena must have left the small brown wooden box for him. "I met your little friend," I tell him dryly. "I don't think he likes me much."

"Ena?" He raises an eyebrow, too intent on inspecting the box to pay me much attention. "He doesn't like anyone. It's why I've kept him on for so long. He senses who a person truly is at their core and compromises himself for no one. There isn't a more honest man in the world."

I swallow hard, recalling his insinuation that I'm nothing more than a toy. "How long has he worked for you?"

"Over a decade," Vadim says offhandedly. "But I've known him longer. Ena is gruff, but I'll make sure he avoids you. Don't worry about him. What you should concern yourself with is this…" He beckons me closer, and I warily comply, coming to stand by his side.

Aware of me watching, he takes his time opening the box, revealing an interior lined with black silk, containing a single, silver object nestled in a specially shaped cavity. It's oval-shaped, about the size of my thumb, and crafted from delicate material.

"What is it?" I ask, unnerved by the bold way he strokes the edge of the container. "I will admit that I was much more impressed by the delivery of a lifetime's worth of Chanel."

Undeterred by my ungratefulness, he reaches into the box and withdraws something else. "This came with it," he explains, revealing a larger, square-shaped object of the same material. The only thing of interest it seems to contain is a silver button built into the center. He presses the button.

A low hum comes from the box as the small object begins to vibrate. Suddenly it clicks, and my thoughts dissipate.

"You ordered this for me?" The mixture of both awe and terror in my voice shocks me almost as much as it seems to please him. His teeth flash, his eyes practically glowing.

"You wanted kink?" he questions, his tone gravelly in a way that makes me shiver. "Let us see if you truly have what it takes. I will admit that I originally didn't have much interest in the subject, but I have started to conduct my own research."

I rock on my heels, my brain spinning, thoughts in disarray. I don't know what shocks me more? The fact that kink was supposedly never on his radar before I goaded him into spanking me, or the fact that...

He's been learning. For me.

"And what have you discovered?" I wonder, batting my eyelashes at him innocently.

That telltale muscle in his jaw twitches, and he lifts the silver vibrator from its box.

"I've learned that control is a defining factor of these... relationships. As is trust. I want to test just how much control you can exert over yourself in the quest for fulfillment. And how much you can trust me to always give you what you need."

No man has ever lived up to the term "panty melting" so thoroughly. The inside of my legs chafe as I take an involuntary step toward him. I don't think I've stopped aching since the office. Boldly, I slip my hand around his neck and sidle up to him, pressing myself against his rigid frame. I'm not the only one aroused. Despite our little oral session, he's straining against my hip. I grind against him slavishly, watching as his eyes glaze over, his tongue tracing his lips.

"You want to sexually torment me?" Again, I sound equally alarmed and excited. I can't keep a tendril of curiosity from my tone either. One little silver dildo has never seemed so intimidating.

"No." He shifts, capturing my chin to force me to face him. "I want to explore your limits. Once I learn them, I can better exploit them."

I suck in a breath. "You aim to *manipulate* me?"

He chuckles and lowers his mouth to my ear. "I aim to pleasure you. More than any other. Do you accept that proposal?"

"So what?" I finger the still vibrating object balanced on his palm and shudder. Even picturing it inside me is…dangerous. "We play with it?"

"No." He steps into me, his stance suddenly clinical, like a doctor about to perform a procedure. "You keep this inside you —" He lowers his hand to my hip, pressing enough for me to feel the vibrations through his skin. *Holy heck.* I grip his forearms for balance, my brain melting. "Until I give you permission to remove it."

I rear back to meet his gaze, my mouth opened in horror. "On?"

"Not constantly." I sense him inhale as he brushes his mouth along my throat, tasting my scent. "However, I will have the remote on me at all times, to be utilized at my discretion. You will be surprised by the range. My main request is that you refrain from touching yourself. At all. Only I may have that privilege. Understood?" His fingers slip beneath my skirt, trailing up my thigh, and I nearly buck into his hand just to find relief.

"So wet," he murmurs in approval. "But this game will not commence tonight. This will be merely the preliminary round."

I frown. "Not even one little orgasm for me?" I arch into him, pressing my breasts against his chest. My hips seem to move of their own accord, grinding, teasing.

With difficulty, he pulls back, leaving only his hand against me. "No," he says thickly. "Do you trust that I will make it good when you finally do experience release?"

Do I trust him? All it takes is the memory of his tongue on me to come up with an answer. "Yes…"

"Good. The other stipulation is that you cannot remove this. I will know if you do."

He guides me back and taking the hint, I lean against the table, spreading my legs. Observing him crouch before me, his head disappearing beneath my skirt is an experience all in itself. Orgasming without touching myself only a few days ago would have seemed like a pipe dream. Now? I arch my back, gasping in anticipation.

My clit is already swollen, demanding attention as the smooth surface of the toy grazes my lips.

Vadim makes a low sound in his throat. "So beautiful you are," he praises. "So eager already. Can you wait for me to savor you?"

I nod, feeling like a child undertaking a chore in the hopes of a treat. And even his slow, careful insertion of the device is a sensual delicacy almost enough to make up for the lack of his fingers. It's so light, I barely feel it, but the vibrations when felt internally…

I grit my teeth, my eyelids fluttering, and my muscles jerk, making me squirm. I'm vaguely aware of him rising to his feet before me, watching my reaction.

Finally, the sensation abates, and I can breathe again.

"Holy…crap…" I'm panting, my body slick with sweat. A wicked grin shapes my mouth even as I contemplate the daunting prospect of enduring this at his discretion for only God knows how long.

"Too unbearable?" Vadim wonders, sounding irritatingly level.

I shake my head. But I can't resist asking, "If I'm a good girl, will you fuck me fast?"

His smile. It's so sinful, so wicked. My toes curl even as my thighs twitch, too aware of the pressure building between them to risk coming together.

"I will fuck you," he promises, copying my filthy language. "All in good time."

I pout, rolling my eyes. "So, what will we do until then?"

"Dinner," he says, smoothly, clearing the table. I note that he tucks the smaller, baby blue box he'd teased me with earlier into his pocket. "It dawned on me as I drove back that I haven't fed you since lunch."

A lunch that we never actually enjoyed, thanks to me.

And I'd been too caught up in the whirlwind day to notice. With a pang of guilt, I recall what Ena said about making him eat. The fact that he seems to take effort on his part to remember normal meal timeframes proves just how little he must eat normally.

"Are you going to cook for me?" I ask as he steps behind the counter and opens the fridge.

"No." He opens a drawer that I assume is the freezer and withdraws a slim, rectangular metal container. The space seems to be full of at least six other similar boxes. After closing the drawer, he places the container on the counter and lifts the lid, revealing a neatly proportioned meal of baked chicken, vegetables, and rice.

"Equestrian. Chef. Damn good in the sack. Is there anything you can't do?" I wonder, partly impressed, partly irritated.

He laughs and places the container in the oven. "I share your thoughts on cooking. You should be complimenting Ena. He continues to make these things for me, though I rarely eat them before they spoil."

"So far, my competition for your heart seems to be against a fake wife, your bodyguard, and a beautiful horse. Can't a girl catch a break?" I'd been speaking without thinking. It's only when I see his jaw clench that I realize how stupidly reckless I was.

Mr. Vadim, the guarded, mistrustful businessman, doesn't seem to want a relationship with me either. Great.

In silence, he opens a cupboard and withdraws two glasses and a familiar bottle of wine. As the food warms, he returns to the table and pours two glasses.

I take a seat across from him and promptly drain over half of my glass in one go. The moment the buzz creeps to my brain, I forget all about my discomfort.

"Why aren't you married?" I ask him, folding my arms before me. "For real?"

He looks away and slips his hand into his pocket. *Zap!* I nearly lunge from my seat as waves of pleasure rip through my core in a relentless, pulsating rhythm. I lose track of everything, trying not to scream as it goes on and on… When it finally relents, I slump against the table, breathless, my chest heaving, nipples erect to the point of pain.

And the bastard is standing before the oven, removing the steaming container. "Food's done," he says. "I hope you have an appetite."

I gape as he divides the food between two plates and places one before me. Smiling, he sits on the opposite end of the table and casually slices off a piece of chicken.

"Don't let the food go cold," he scolds.

I eat warily, constantly on edge. My mother once tried fence training her Pomeranian with a shock collar, and in this moment, I feel for the poor thing. Only more wine can soothe my nerves.

"Dinner with your brother is in two days," I point out, sounding breathless. "What happens after that?"

He shrugs and chews on a bit of vegetables. "I have many talents, but I'm afraid that seeing into the future isn't one of them."

My upper lip quirks even as real irritation sears through my nerves. Bastard. "It looks like you're learning to have a sense of humor, at least."

He smiles, one of those rare, authentic grins. Again, I can't shake the sense that whatever happened today changed him. Shook something loose in him that leaves him sitting languidly, clearing his plate for the first time since I've been with him. Maybe it was going to the stables? I let him show me something special to him.

And now I only want more. Another sip of wine firmly shoves me from borderline tipsy into drunk territory, giving me the courage to probe him despite the risk of sexual torture.

"If I wanted to stay after the dinner, what would you bribe me with?"

I'm boasting, of course. There's no way I'm actually considering it. Not even as his eyes cut up to mine, darkly suspicious.

"What would you want?"

"Hmm…" I mull it over, making him wait. "Tell me what *merde* means," I say, picking a harmless target first.

Those dark eyes fixate on me mercilessly. "It could be translated as 'shit,'" he finally admits, taking another bite of his food—seconds. "An expression of frustration, you might say."

And one he seems to love spilling around me. I puff up, oddly pleased to have pushed him to such a breaking point. Cursing doesn't seem like his go-to vice. I've made him utilize it.

"What about *ta gueule?*" I ask, no doubt butchering the phrase he'd hissed at me while in the club.

"It means 'shut up.' Is that all you want?" he prods before I can retort, his tone mocking. "Translations?"

"No." I meet his gaze and lick my lips. "You buy me a horse as magnificent as Zzazza so that we can have an honest race between us to settle who the better rider is, once and for all. I have a feeling you'll be the one to *'ta gueule.'*"

He laughs, his eyes sparkling. "If such a creature existed, I would have no trouble procuring him for you."

"When did you get her?" I ask, presumably another easy topic.

But I'm wrong.

His face falls, his wall erected in a heartbeat. "When I was lost," he says softly. "On the verge of death. She…she brought me back to life."

"Oh." I want to ask him more. I bounce in my seat, weighing the risk. Screw it. I start to, "Tell me—"

"We should head to bed." He stands and grabs our plates and—sadly—wine glasses and places them in the sink.

"I'll help." I grudgingly rise and cross over to assist.

Bzzzz. I howl and grasp the counter, my legs turning to jelly as searing pleasure builds, fed by incredible friction. No matter how tightly I clamp my legs, it builds. Builds. It's almost too much, going on for too long. Pleasure turns sharp, honed to a painful, aching need, and I have to physically stop myself from reaching into my panties just to find some relief.

Finally, it stops, and I'm on my knees, shaking against the side of the counter.

"I'll meet you in bed," Vadim says, strolling for the staircase at a leisurely pace. "Ten minutes should be enough time for you to prepare, correct?"

Prepare? "But where am I going to sleep—"

A teasing jolt has me yelping though it only lasts a second. A warning, I suspect. Its intention is clear—I'm sleeping with him. In his bed. Again.

When I'm able to walk without staggering, I practically run up the stairs and into the bedroom. My cheeks heat as I pass him stripping beside the bed, and I enter the closet, grabbing a more conservative bit of lingerie—a black negligée. Then I race into the bathroom, wash up—dragging a cloth gingerly between my legs—and I finally approach the bed with minutes to spare of my deadline.

Yawning for his benefit, I wrench back the covers and climb onto the mattress beside him as if I'm not intimidated by the idea at all.

Sleeping beside him without the aid of a lusty stupor to explain it.

Sighing, he copies me, but he doesn't remain on his end for long. Shock runs through me as his hand lands over my hip, wrenching me against him. Effortlessly, he folds over me from behind, preventing any hope of shimmying away during the night. It's the most dangerous concept of spooning one could ever envision.

"Goodnight, *baby*," he murmurs against my scalp. "Try your very best to get some sleep."

And I go alight with the threat.

CHAPTER EIGHTEEN

Vadim Gorgoshev is a sadist.

I barely drift off before I'm jolting awake, gasping in agony. Those vibrations return with a vengeance, ten times more intense, given how sensitive I already am. What felt like a nine on the pleasure scale before is cranked up to twenty.

I'm gasping to smother any moans, writhing beneath the sheets. Nearby, a sturdier body lies innocently motionless, even as a moan finally succeeds in escaping my throat. Moisture coats my inner thighs, spiking the air. Despite my neighbor's rigid stance, I sense him inhale—even in my addled state.

And it somehow adds to the building inferno like gasoline.

I'm trembling when the pleasure finally eases.

Cautiously, I fall asleep.

Only to be startled awake again.

Over.

Over.

Over again.

I lose track of how many times it happens through the night. Enough that I'm barely coherent when dawn light displaces the shadows, and Vadim moves from his spot, looking infuriatingly refreshed.

"Sleep well?" he inquires before strolling toward the bathroom.

I can't even answer. I'm too busy contemplating how much shame I'd feel if I admitted defeat right in this moment and rubbed myself off. I never knew that arousal could be this painful. This…intense. My clit is my brain's sole focus, demanding relief. Anything.

"I have work at the office," Vadim says, returning fully dressed. His crisp ebony suit bolsters the reality that it's already late in the morning. I'm losing track of time, my brain is so scrambled. "I don't know how late I'll be," he adds, drawing my attention back to him.

I suck in a breath as he leans down and plants a kiss on my sweaty forehead.

"I will see you later tonight."

My heart lurches. "T-Tonight?"

He leaves the room without a reply, but I don't trust my legs to attempt to follow. I shimmy to the edge of the mattress instead and tentatively brace my foot on the floor. *Buzz!* Another torrent of vibration makes me curl into a ball, and I scream for real. Fuck him. God, I want to. I need to. I can't…

Think.

Desperate for some kind of distraction, I stumble into the bathroom and try to shower.

Buzz.

Buzz.

Buzz.

It's too much, and I wind up trembling naked on the cool marble floor, seeking out what little comfort I can find. My body is a slave to my libido, heightened to an insane degree. Something about the toy's design must make it so the pleasure provided is incredible—but never *quite* enough stimulation for an orgasm. The result is some hellish sexual purgatory.

And at the back of my mind, I'm praising Vadim as a horrible sexual genius asshole—I got my wish. Debouched kink times a thousand.

My nipples are rock-hard, my hair matted with sweat, my thoughts sluggish. My only remaining goal is to not get myself off. Even if it means I cry in torment, feeling real tears stream down my face as the toy buzzes. On. Off. Again.

The bastard wasn't lying about the range of his remote. It's like I can time each bout, using what I witnessed of his schedule yesterday as a guide. He's read his newspapers. Remembered me. Struck his button. Drank his orange juice and ate his breakfast. Button. Drove to the office. Button. Went through reports. Button.

Button.

Button.

I know I can't survive another fucking minute when the sensation has me wavering between lucidity and utter insanity. If I somehow manage to reach a phone and call him, would he come? But I won't. Fuck him and his game. This torture. In defiance, I crawl back to the bed and climb onto the mattress, guiding my hand down my belly. But something won't let me bridge that final inch.

And as if sensing my flirtation with rebellion, Vadim hits his fucking button.

I'm senseless, screaming. Cursing. I don't even hear the thud of quickly approaching footsteps until their source is standing over me, his voice a gentle hum.

"*Merde…* Are you aching for me?"

It's like my brain is torn in half. The first part can only register his scent. His nearness. I unfurl my limbs and nearly jump from the bed onto him. He's wearing a black suit, and I clumsily rip at the fabric of his pants.

The other half registers the genuine awe in his voice—mingled with that ever-present suspicion. The latter lasts only as long as it takes me to claw at the fastenings of his pants.

"My beauty." His voice alone enhances my torment, in addition to the reverent way he strokes my damp hair and tries to meet my gaze. It's too much. Too much intimacy in this moment. He's having another revelation, but I'm too far gone to wonder about what.

To care.

"P-Please." I can barely speak, my voice high-pitched and broken. "Vadim, please—"

"Lie back." He brushes my hands away and quickly unfastens his pants himself. My entire body rocks at the sight of his cock.

Pulsing, completely erect, so thick, I can't imagine how he's not as mindless as I am. Though maybe he is… A muscle in his jaw twitches, his eyelids lowering as I spread my legs.

"Incredible," he grates—real, unforced praise. With his gaze fixated between my thighs, he mounts the bed and slides his hand between my legs. I nearly levitate as his fingers enter me, focused on a task other than providing pleasure. There must be some trick to removing the toy, requiring a gentle, teasing bit of manipulation. Then, he yanks, ripping the device free, and I howl with relief. The next second I'm splayed beneath him, and he's finally easing inside me.

My eyes roll back into my head as I convulse amid a sensation too intense to name at first. *Electric. Punishing pleasure.* One orgasm quickly blends into another. Another. Another. All I can do is cling to him and ride every dizzying wave, sobbing his name until I lose my voice altogether.

I never knew it was possible to crave someone so much. To feel so much hedonistic gratification, it becomes unbearable. Agonizing.

It's only when he rears back and slides his hands beneath me that I realize he hasn't moved since that first thrust. His eyes meet mine, his lips parting, voice relentless.

"You waited for me, didn't you?" Again, he sounds thoroughly shaken. As if he's come to some massive, world-altering conclusion. Something that I think should terrify me. All I can do is rasp his name in confirmation.

I waited.

And he pulsates, his jaw clenched. "You knew that only I could ever give you this." His eyes darken as he grips my hips and snatches me to him.

I moan, my back arching, toes curling. How is it possible to be filled so completely? The sensation floods up through my body, straining my very skin. I'm bursting at the seams, so weak that I'm helpless when he rocks his hips and thrusts again.

Again.

He moves hungrily, grunting, his eyes fluttering shut as he goes deep. Deeper. Fathomlessly deep.

It's more than I can take. All coherent thoughts vanish beneath a wave of ecstasy so potent that I know with a horrifying certainty that no one else could ever give me this. It's the insanity brought on by the toy talking. Inspiring this crazed understanding that no one else will ever feel this good. I would never let anyone else reduce me to this.

I praise him wordlessly, driven by an instinct I can't name to stave off the next release I feel building. Not until I sense him stiffen, his cock pulsating inside of me, his voice a throaty rasp.

"You will come with me," he commands as if reading my mind, connected to me in every way. "Come for me, beauty."

And I do so screaming.

His release floods me like an antidote to a pain I didn't even realize had been festering inside me. I surrender to him, letting him fuck out the rest of his release until we both collapse in a boneless mass. His arms encircle me, dragging me against his chest so that my head rests against his shoulder as I gasp to catch my breath.

It's a slow, surreal descent from cloud nine. I can't stop shaking as my body registers normal sensations again. The coolness of the room. The heat of him. The fact that the sunlight streaming in through the windows betrays that it's either late in the morning or early in the afternoon.

So much for him returning tonight. A cocky smile quirks my lips —I wasn't the only one in agony, it seems.

"Are you alright?" Real concern edges his tone as he strokes my arm, sensing every quaking twitch of my muscles. He sounds so hesitating, truly worried for me.

With what little strength I can muster, I tilt my head back to meet his worried gaze. Once he sees my expression, his lips part into a dazzling grin.

Panting, I tell him, "Best…idea…ever."

CHAPTER NINETEEN

We sleep for what feels like an eternity but turns out to only be a few hours before hunger drives me awake. I roll over to face him only to find him already watching me through hooded eyes.

"I love the way you sleep," he declares, his voice a shallow rasp.

My aching pussy throbs, and I groan, so sensitive that even his voice seems liable to set me off.

"I love the way you come for me," he adds mercilessly, teasing his fingers through my hair. "I love the way you sound. And...I love that you trusted me to pleasure you."

I sigh, my lips stuck in what seems like a permanent, if tired, grin. "You are affectionate when you're sprung," I tease him, my voice hoarse. Gently, I stroke his chest, marveling at the softness of his skin. "I love the toy you had made for me. I love the game we played—"

"Enough to do it again?" he wonders, an eyebrow raised.

An ominous shiver runs through me as I decide upon my answer. Yes. I would. Turning into him, I brush my lips along his collar, tasting him. "I want to play many games with you."

"Your wish is my command." His smug tone warns me that the vibrator wasn't his only custom-made item in the works. Does that scare me?

"You are excited," Vadim suspects, stroking my chin. "Does my kink please you?"

I roll onto my back and languidly stretch out my sore, aching limbs. "I *love* your kink. But I really need to shower, and I'm starving." I crawl toward the end of the mattress, but he stands before I even make it halfway.

"No." Stern steps bring him to my side. Before I know it. I'm in his arms, cradled to his chest. "You are to be pampered," he says while carrying me into the bathroom.

My grin grows wider. "Is that what you learned from your research?"

His wicked smirk warms me more than the temperature he sets the shower to before setting me onto a marble bench built into the wall of the stall.

"My research has taught me many things," he explains as he returns to my side, laden with bottles of luxurious looking bath soap and fresh washcloths. "That you are to be pampered and rested in between our games, for one—" He lathers up a cloth with the sweetest smelling soap I've ever smelled and washes my legs, starting at each ankle. "And that I am to never push you too far. And that ensuring your pleasure should be my main desire. *Never* to hurt you."

I swipe my fingers through his wet hair, loving the feel of it. Like silk.

"It seems I'm in good hands," I say, spreading my legs so that he can continue his ministrations unabated.

The man takes his time, bathing every inch of me until I feel so boneless, I doubt I could walk on my own. Not that I'm given the choice to. He dries us off with a towel and then carries me back into the room. With a secretive smile, he sets me on the freshly made mattress before he wanders into the closet. A few minutes later, he returns dressed in a pair of sweatpants and with one of my less revealing nightgowns—an ivory one made of silk—slung over his arm.

The man even dresses me, resisting any attempt I make to help.

"I will bring you food," he explains as he pads to the door, leaving me splayed on the bed.

"More food of Ena's?" I playfully taunt.

He chuckles rather than answer.

And I go to war within myself. This is going too far. Too fast. An intimate bath and breakfast in bed take this liaison far beyond a one-night stand. The fact that we're well beyond one night makes that clear as well. I should be doing whatever it takes to cement the boundary between us, and when I hear his steps approach, I'm ready to remind him of the unescapable facts—this won't last. It certainly isn't real. I need to return to California.

But then he rounds the corner, strolling through the doorway, and I forget my train of thought.

"From your stunned silence, I can assume this meal is to your liking?" he wonders innocently while advancing sporting a silver tray piled high with sweets and delicacies on one hand while holding a bottle of wine in the other.

The good wine.

Too stunned to argue, I scoot over to make room, and it isn't long before I'm eating right from his hands. I groan with utter content as I sample a chocolate-covered strawberry.

"I *love* when you pamper me," I declare as my eyes glaze over.

He chuckles, and his fingers dance over the tray of desserts in search of another treat. "I'm beginning to suspect that chocolate is your weakness every bit as much as wine is."

I nod, relaxing into him. He sits with his back to the headboard while I lie in between his legs, leaning against his chest. Spoiled, tipsy, and with my brain still mush from earlier, I'm in no state to filter myself.

"What made you come after me?" I ask, thinking back to that night at the club. My teeth descend into my lower lip as I picture it. The very first time I pushed him past his boundaries with marvelous results. "I thought I wasn't your type?"

"You aren't." He's frowning even as he says it. Before I can fully tense, he lowers his mouth to my ear, his breaths thick and hesitant. "Maybe that's a good thing... Or bad," he adds, "considering my finances."

A self-satisfied grin tugs on the corner of my mouth. "Tell me."

He sighs as if thinking it over. Then he picks a small, bite-sized piece of cake from his tray and brings it to my mouth. As I chew, he says, "You challenged me." His tone deepens, making it sound so novel to him. A foreign concept. "I've offended women before. Some left. Others threaten to ruin me, or extort me for money..." His eyes take on a cold gleam, betraying that sadistic hint of his personality. I pity the poor woman that ever thought she could take advantage of him. Something tells me, he more than ensured they regretted that decision. He relished in it. But then he cocks his head, his mouth tilted downward. "None have ever threatened to compare my sexual prowess to that of a sex club's full roster before," he admits, brushing his finger along my exposed shoulder.

I shrug to hide my blushing cheeks. "Could you see yourself wanting a real relationship with a woman you don't have to bribe?"

Beneath me, his chest rumbles with a thoughtful hum. "Could you see yourself in a relationship so soon after your divorce?"

I squirm, unnerved by how easily he saw to my main source of hesitation.

"I don't know," I admit. "In theory, I want to say no, but in practice? I suppose there could be someone out there worth exploring something deeper with, no matter the time frame."

And yet, I'm frowning. The thought is surprisingly unnerving, far too serious for my drunken brain to contemplate, so I crane my neck back and open my mouth.

Taking the hint, he places an exquisite looking piece of chocolate onto my tongue. I groan, sufficiently distracted, all thoughts of losing my newfound independence forgotten.

"Do you ever see yourself getting married again?" Vadim asks, unwilling to let the subject drop.

Damn. I take my time swallowing and then shrug. "I don't know—"

"What about children?" His voice shifts, taking on a deeper, more cautious tone. Something about his reaction triggers a part of my brain, but I'm not sure why. Maybe recognition? It's the same wistful, guttural way he spoke about his horse, betraying a deeper emotion I can't comprehend just yet.

Which leads to a more important question—does he want children?

"No. I... I don't want children," I confess. If I did want to pursue a relationship with anyone, it's best to get that out of the way. "I don't."

He stiffens, and my cheeks catch fire. It's the same reaction I've grown used to, and one of the main reasons why I've avoided my parents, in addition to loathing their guilt.

Your biological clock is ticking, Tiffy, they gently remind at every opportunity. *You don't want to be alone forever. You would make a wonderful mother.*

"It's not like I hate children," I add in a rush. "I love them. So, so much. I always wanted to be a mother too, but when I was with Jim..." I close my eyes, combating an unexpected prickling sensation—that of tears threatening to form. "He was kind of a Nazi when it came to setting the timeline of when he thought we were 'ready.' In short, never. He'd spin the tired old excuses about having enough money or time, but the truth was he never wanted a baby. Not with me, anyway. But as these things usually happen, I got pregnant unexpectedly." I suck in a breath as the pain rises up swiftly, striking like a punch to the chest.

"You don't have to say anymore," Vadim warns, still cradling me in his arms. Maybe it's his warmth that makes me brave enough to keep talking?

"I was so happy," I croak. "Everyone says that, but I can't explain… I truly was so ecstatic. My relationship with Jim was a bust, but with this new baby? I would be the perfect mother. I would do anything…"

"What happened?" Vadim prompts, his voice soft. I look down, surprised to find that he grabbed my hand without my realizing it. His thumb strokes my palm, and I find that it's easier to continue now—when I've never spoken about this to anyone. Not my one-time therapist. Not my parents. Not even Jim.

"I have some pre-existing medical issues, so I knew it was a risk from the start. I prayed for a healthy pregnancy, anyway," I add thickly. "I promised that I would be perfect, just as long as everything went well. Jim wasn't happy, but for the first time, I didn't give a damn what he thought. I was happy. I was confident I could do it alone if I had to, and that was enough. But…" I sigh, and tears fall, impossible to keep at bay. "I woke up one morning, barely four weeks in, and I knew something was wrong. I went to the hospital, they told me there was no heartbeat, and… I can't explain what that felt like. I can't. I don't think anyone can ever understand unless you sit there watching some stupid machine refuse to pick up what you know in your heart should be there. It's devastating. It is world-altering. But at the back of my mind, I always knew that it was probably a blessing. I couldn't do it. I wasn't ready."

Case and point? Jim got the privilege of becoming a parent before I ever could—a "fuck you" from the universe if there ever was one.

Vadim's silent, but I suspect he's thinking again, mulling over the best way to phrase his next question. "You've never considered adoption?"

I shake my head. "I had a friend—well, a member of the church —who adopted through foster care, and it was a magical experience. That is until the drug-addicted mother attended a few classes and decided she wanted her baby back. All it took was one overzealous judge to mandate visitation, and the adoption was undone. I can't go through that pain. I can't…"

"I'm sorry."

Something in my heart rips open, and I can't stop the vicious onslaught of tears. His judgment I could handle. Maybe a scoff, or an eye roll, or a gentle reminder that loss happens and I should get over it or some bullshit like what my therapist—who lasted a week—tried to shove down my throat. His understanding is a balm on an infected, blistering wound, and it burns like disinfectant.

"What about you?" I croak, wiping at my eyes. "Are children in your future?"

He goes rigid again, and I shiver as his fingers trace a path up to my wrist. "Too personal? I'm sorry—"

"I was abused as a child." He says it so tonelessly that it takes my brain a second to process it. When I do, horror washes over me so heavy I can't suppress it. I gasp. A million of his little nuances flash through my mind, cementing his claim. His piercing. His mistrust. His initial approach to sex.

And I suddenly feel like the biggest bitch in the world for pushing him. Taunting him. Dragging him from his comfort zone without a damn given to anyone but myself.

"Oh, baby…" I reach for him, lacing my fingers with his free hand.

"I won't go into the details," he adds, his tone eerily level. Robotic almost. "But whatever form or manner you can envision happened, most likely did."

I twist around and stroke his jaw, my eyes brimming with even more tears. He looks so cool again, so distant. But this time, his wall is down, and I can sense the monstrous effort on his part that must take. To let me in. To allow me to feel the tension rippling through him.

"Children of my own was never something I envisioned." A cold, slow smile shapes his mouth. "But it seems the universe enjoys taunting me by challenging my past perceptions."

"How?" I ask hoarsely.

He shakes his head—a topic for another day, I suspect.

"You'd make an amazing father." I sound mournful as I admit it. To gauge his reaction, I turn around as I sink against him. "You're patient. Gentle…"

"You can be so sure despite knowing me for only a week?" he questions skeptically, throwing his arm over my hip.

I nod. "Yes. Call it my special gift—" Either that or a major character flaw. "I'm good at reading people. *Too* good. I knew within two days that Jim was a self-centered, abrasive asshole. I just ignored the warning signs. But you? I find myself trying harder just to ignore the *good* things. So yes, I have no doubt that you'd make an amazing dad."

Given the empathy evident in how he cared for his horse alone, a child of his would grow up both spoiled and cherished beyond measure. And he deserves a woman who could give him that future.

"I've upset you," he says as I roll off of him.

"No." I shake my head as I climb from the bed and stand on shaking legs. "I'm fine. I promise."

I just feel the need to put distance between us, any way I can. I wind up in the bathroom, slumping over the counter. My eyes are bloodshot, my bottom lip trembling. Self-pity?

No. The pain ripping through my chest has everything to do with guilt. Vadim is such an infuriatingly stubborn, guarded, mysterious man. And the more time I spend around him, the more of him I'm starting to crave. My instincts are warning me to run far and fast. Before it's too late and I do something stupid.

Like jump into another relationship with someone I barely know.

I splash cool water onto my face and then reenter the bedroom with a lazy grin. He's still propped up in bed, watching me warily.

"Are you alright?"

"Yes." I skip to his end of the bed and climb onto the mattress— directly onto him. He grunts in shock, capturing my waist to keep me steady. I plant a drunk kiss on his jaw and keep kissing my way down his chest until the tension drains from him completely.

"I love being with you," I confess, somewhere near his navel. "May your future fake wife burn in hell."

He leans back and meets my gaze, an eyebrow raised. "Is this your way of telling me that you plan on escaping after tomorrow night?"

"Tomorrow?" Belatedly I remember dinner with his brother, my supposed reason for staying this long. "I guess our arrangement will be over, then."

"Will it?" That dangerous gleam ignites in his gaze, setting the hairs on the back of my neck on end. "You've been so intent on leaving that you have yet to ask yourself—will I let you go? I think you might very much enjoy bondage play."

Excitement bubbles in my belly at the mere thought of having him shackle me. *Snap out of it, Tiffy.*

"You won't want me around for very long," I say, shifting my position to nuzzle his neck. "One month of my spending, and you'll cancel your fancy card and send my ass right back to California."

"I doubt that." His voice deepens into a richer, thicker baritone and my toes curl in response. "I've had more entertainment watching you squeal in excitement over a few dresses than I've ever experienced through my wealth.

"Mmm." I purr, wiggling against him. "Keep talking dirty to me, and I may let you play with that damn toy again." I spare a glance at the hated object, resting on his nightstand, freshly cleaned.

"Dirty?" he echoes, pressing me against him. "Stay with me after tomorrow night, and I will show you the world I could offer you."

My breath catches as my brain spins with a million possibilities. More shopping sprees. More carefree mornings. More impromptu horse rides and casual dinners. An abundance of kinky sex.

"You are considering it," he accuses while laughing that buttery laugh.

"I am," I confess. "But you shouldn't want me to. I think I might be…bad for you." I frown, even as I say it. A selfish part of me wants to immediately take the words back. Why can't I chase him, even if our ultimate aims aren't compatible? Maybe I could change my mind. Maybe…

"Bad for me?" He laughs in that sinful way, and his hands creep up my ribcage, cupping my breasts. He groans as my nipples harden and traces their peeks through the fabric of my negligee. "You have been terrible for me—" He flicks his gaze up to mine, watching my reaction. Something in his heated expression makes me suspect he didn't intend the confession as an insult. "I've been distracted from my work. Rather than just a few hours at a time, I find that I've been sleeping through the night these past few days. Not to mention, I'm considering meeting Maxim *without* the aid of an armed guard. You have thoroughly demolished my routine. I'm sure you are pleased with yourself."

My grin returns wider than ever. "So pleased." I brush my lips over his, relishing the feel of him. He's so soft, but so dominating the second he pushes back, urging my lips apart for his tongue to slip between.

The kiss is sweet at first. Then hungrier until I'm lying naked beneath him, and he's palming his cock, his eyes unfocused, our breathing labored.

I part my legs, and he easily sinks inside me.

One thrust takes me so high I go right past cloud nine and straight up to ten.

And even as I quake amid the aftermath, I know that I'm already well past the danger zone of becoming addicted to him.

CHAPTER TWENTY

I wake up in his arms, and we spend most of the morning lying in bed, talking about nothing in particular. It's surprisingly easy to share his space and enjoy his nearness. I could never pass time like this with Jim. Not that he would give me the time of day regardless.

Vadim? He acts as though his business and unknown meetings can wait. As if letting me nuzzle at his throat is worth more than anything else. And the giddy, childish joy goes straight to my head.

"When will you pierce me?" I wonder, nestling against his chest.

A low, shocked grunt resonates from his throat. "You are eager for it?"

I purr and nod, surprised by that fact almost as much as he seems to be. "I'm *so* eager for it. I'm sure you have it all planned out, and I like where your brain goes when you 'research.'"

He chuckles, his gaze thoughtful. "I think you will enjoy the ultimate result, but I am not quite ready yet."

I pout. Then I remember the looming deadline that is tonight, and some of my giddiness diminishes. "Ena warned me about you," I admit. "He said that your brother makes you crazy, and that I am just a toy in whatever is going on between you two."

"Is that so?" His tired sigh ruffles my hair, and he gently smooths the stray strands back into place. "Ena is…let's just say, protective of me. He has earned that right. But I have learned that eighty-percent of the time, he's as overzealous as a worrisome mother."

"And the other twenty percent?" I ask.

His mouth twitches into a reluctant frown. "While he may be overzealous, he is usually never wrong. In this case, I believe precedent may be coloring his perception—" He runs his hand down my back as if in reassurance. "Maxim brings out the worst in me, and Ena knows that better than most."

"How did you meet him?" I inquire next as I trace a path from one perfect nipple to the other. "He doesn't strike me as the type to stroll into one of your offices wearing a suit with a resume tucked under his arm."

"No." His second sigh resonates through my skin, more wistful than the first. "He saved my life. And I don't mean it in the sense that he stopped a bullet for me, or prevented my murder—which he has, many times. I mean it in the most primal sense of the phrase. He saved my life. I met him at a time when I had nothing. Was nothing. For that reason, I will always humor his quirks. Though I may have to remind him that not everyone is so tolerant of his bluntness."

"Tell me?" I risk asking even as he stiffens, his gaze turning distant. "I know I'm prying—and if you don't want to, I won't push it. But I want to know. I'm willing to listen."

I sense his wall wavering, threatening to solidify against me. Driven by an impulse I can't name, I brush my fingers through his hair and cradle his jaw. Finally, he blinks. When his gaze fixates on mine again, it's more intense than ever.

"I was property once," he says bluntly. "Take that as you may. I can't…" He swallows hard, shaking his head. "Some things I won't relive in full. Do you still want to hear it?"

"Yes," I croak without an ounce of hesitation. "I'll listen to whatever you're willing to tell."

"I was property," he repeats. "Little more than a slave but without the benefit of even that title. My worth registered in the tens of thousands, and yet at my core? I was worthless. Soulless. I was nothing."

My heart pounds as an ominous foreboding makes me settle against him, pressing my ear to his chest. Despite the obvious pain in his voice, his heartbeat is sluggishly slow. Too slow. As if his body is completely disconnected from the horror in his mind. Tremors ripple through him, reminding me of the way he shook around Maxim. It's like he's freezing from the inside out, even as his skin blazes.

"My last 'owner' possessed acres of property in some European country, untouchable by the authorities. They called him 'the collector' and he more than lived up to that name. Animals. Weapons. Vehicles…people. He loved horses, you see. He had stables filled with them. And when things got unbearable, they were my escape."

The detachedness of his voice creates a horrific picture. One so sickening, I can't even envision it fully—a nightmare far beyond my picturesque upbringing in southern California.

"The bastard would send his goons after me, and more often than not, I'd be severely punished," Vadim says. "But for whatever reason, when all else in life had lost any appeal, that haven remained tempting enough for me to risk seeking it out at every opportunity. One horse, in particular, drew my notice. A young filly who the stable hands had deemed 'incorrigible'—" He smiles in that rare, genuine way that makes my heart ache. "She retained her spirit despite their attempts to break her, and was prone to lashing out and biting."

"Zzazza?" I say softly.

He nods. "She never attacked me. Not even the first night I snuck into her stall to hide, bloodied, and broken. Whenever anyone came by looking for me, she'd snarl and bite, but never at me."

"How did you escape?"

"One day, my 'owner' decided that I was a liability worth eliminating. He had me beaten within an inch of my life and called in one of his guards to finish the job..." Something terrible constricts his features. A raw pain, unlike anything I've ever witnessed. The type of agony that can only be experienced to understand—a loss of yourself. "I begged for my life," he confesses hoarsely. "Like an animal, I begged. Pleaded. Sobbed. I will never understand why then—I had been through worse before. Never once did I plead. But I did, even though I knew the guard would laugh and kill me anyway. I had resigned myself to death. But I was wrong..." He frowns as if still stunned by that fact. "The guard aimed his gun at me, and then turned it on my bastard owner and pulled the trigger. There was no hesitation in him. No ounce of wavering or struggle. He merely made a decision, and that was that. He helped me escape, and since then, he has never made a decision I do not trust."

I swallow hard, my eyes burning. "So maybe I can try to be nice to Ena a little," I say with a watery laugh.

"He is one of the few men I trust in the world," Vadim swears. "And he makes a mean chocolate cake if you do manage to get in his good graces."

"Ah, so the man prefers chocolate as well," I say, filing away the fact for later.

"I enjoy many things," he says, sliding his arms around my waist, drawing me even closer. Near my ear, he murmurs, "Many of them new revelations."

"Such as?" I wonder smugly.

"Such as kink," he says, his voice deepening. "I never knew sex could be so…stimulating."

My breathing hitches. I can't shake his previous confession. Did I really push him too far?

"In a good way," he adds before I can fear the worst. "It can be… pleasurable." He pauses as if fighting to find the right words. "I am not used to that experience."

And yet, he hires escorts seemingly on a regular basis. Does the lack of connection—paired with his obvious joy of manipulation —make it easier for him, even if pleasure isn't his main goal? It's an admittedly cold way to approach such an intimate act. No wonder he'd been so alarmed by my enthusiasm the first night we met.

"I never knew that research could be involved," he adds with a rasping laugh. "That, too, I have come to enjoy."

My grin expands across my face. "Do you *love* our kink?"

"With you, I do. I may even come to love your filthy mouth. The things you say."

"Little me?" I turn to face him and flutter my eyelashes. "I would never say anything vulgar! Like that, I really, really want you to fuck me. Now. Hard."

His eyes narrow as he snatches me to him and promptly rolls over, trapping me beneath him. "Challenge accepted."

CHAPTER TWENTY-ONE

Far too soon, night starts to fall, and we reluctantly leave the safety of the bed for reality. He enters the shower while I comb through the closet and compile two outfits muted in nature—a black suit for him, and an ebony dress for me—fashioned with a modest neckline this time.

I pick out his tie as he gets dressed, and I approach him cautiously, looping it around his neck. "Nervous?" I ask, trying to make my tone more joking than serious.

His eyes darken, gazing into space beyond me. "You asked me once why I did it," he says, his voice so cold I shiver as I twist the tie in on itself. "Why I brought you across the country just for a dinner. Why? You were unpredictable." He slowly lowers his eyes to meet mine. "In my world, those who subvert my expectations have been the only ones I can trust... Don't assume my sole reason was to humiliate you."

I digest the confession slowly, swallowing hard. "I guess I should take that as a compliment, then?"

But I don't. Ena. Zzazza. It feels far more than normal praise to join the ranks of those precious few. Far more vital—and terrifying. I'm getting the sense that those Vadim deems worthy of his attention don't leave his orbit so easily. Like his brother…

"Did Maxim subvert your expectations, too?" I ask softly. Gosh, I can't even look at him. Psychoanalyzing someone like him is a dangerous game to play—but it makes sense. A man so calculating doesn't waste his effort on those who he feels aren't worth the time, family or not.

Not even if they flirt with his hateful side more than most.

Rather than reply, I sense his finger graze my cheek in a simple, lingering caress. When he withdraws, I'm shivering more violently than before. "Get dressed."

Once I'm ready, we head down to the car, and I sense a shift the second he claims the driver's seat beside me. The wall is back up, and the contrast in his demeanor is stark—his eyes darken, his knuckles white as he grips the steering wheel tightly.

"I wonder what's on the menu?" I say in a last-ditch attempt to spark some of the previous humor that had bubbled between us only a few hours ago.

He doesn't laugh or respond, for that matter. I suspect he didn't even hear me. He sits stiffly, hunched over the wheel, his jaw clenched in stubborn silence.

"Baby?" I touch his shoulder, surprised to find him shaking. "Vadim—"

"I'm fine." He shrugs me off, and I choke down any other attempts at conversation, turning my attention to the road. Rather than his brother's house, we head toward the city and eventually arrive before a familiar, impressive building.

The kinky sex club. A strange place to have a family dinner, that's for damn sure. Rather than say as much out loud, I follow him inside. It doesn't register until I spot the familiar surroundings of dark walls and floors that this is the same bar I entered—only now, it's been completely rearranged.

Gone are the scantily clad patrons and oodles of sensual atmosphere. Instead, a long dining table dominates the center of the room, set for six. The tall man, Milton, stands to greet us, followed by the beautiful blond from the party as well.

I sheepishly offer my contribution—one of my precious bottles of vintage. "We brought wine." I make my smile as wide and charming as I'm physically able to. The blond hides her answering grin.

But no one else even cracks a smirk. Still, I take it as a small win. At least *someone* has a sense of normal dinner-party etiquette.

Vadim's brother remains seated beside his young fiancée. His eyes fixate on us, narrowed to slits. Even while dressed in a suit, he radiates feral energy that makes it shockingly easy to picture him lunging across the table at any moment, fists poised to deal out a blow.

"You had the nerve to show up," he growls, his accent thick, his voice booming. "I thought proposing this fucking farce was an elaborate joke on Milton's part."

"What can I say?" Vadim shrugs, and a cruel smile replaces his playful one. "You could have always rescinded the invitation, dear Maxim," he counters.

"It wasn't his bloody invitation to rescind," Milton cuts in, eyeing Maxim with a heated stare fit to light a fire. "Please, sit."

I follow Vadim's lead, taking the seat beside him. As I look up, I realize that we're on an island unto ourselves. Everyone else is seated on the opposite end.

"This looks lovely," I rasp, eyeing the steaming trays of food placed at intervals throughout the length of the table. Roasted meat. Vegetables. My fingers twitch as I spot my bottle of wine, but I suppress the urge to lunge for it.

This isn't about me or my nerves. They're nothing in comparison to the man beside me. He's still shaking, and real concern makes me grasp his hand, squeezing tight. Sweat beads across his forehead, and Ena's warning invades my thoughts. When was the last time he's eaten?

"You have some damn nerve coming here, I will give you that," Maxim snarls, palming the table. His hands are massive, the knuckles scarred and battered. "Did he tell you?" He turns his piercing gaze to me, and I flinch, sliced through. "Did little Dima mention that he kidnapped a child. Held her hostage while her sister panicked, thinking the worst. Did he tell you that?"

Alarmed, I look at Vadim, and I barely recognize him. He's ice-cold, his wall an ocean between us. The skeptical, twisted part of my brain races through the reasons why someone might kidnap a little girl—none of them heartwarming. Especially when paired with what he mentioned of his past...

"Did he?" Maxim presses, his tone so fierce I can't resist replying.

"No," I admit hoarsely. "He didn't tell me that."

"And did he tell you that he threatened my life? That he likes to play God with his money? That he is a snake—"

"What a lovely dinner," Vadim says, his grin wicked. He pushes back from the table and stands. "I'm afraid I'll have to take my leave—"

"I'm not done with you." Maxim lurches to his feet as well. "Did you tell your whore that she is nothing more than a puppet in your quest to mock me?"

The woman beside Maxim lowers her head as my cheeks catch fire. I feel slapped. My lips are already parting as I attempt to stammer out a reply.

But another voice cuts over me. "Enough." Very softly, Vadim murmurs, "I suggest you choose your words more carefully, Maxim. Whore is a strong word to use in your circumstances."

The brunette's eyes blaze, her chin set stubbornly, and Maxim rocks onto the balls of his feet, opening his stance.

"Get the hell out."

Milton stands then, "*Maxim*—"

"Gladly." Vadim snatches my wrist, yanking me to my feet. "We were just leaving—"

"Good. I hope you've had your fun playing copycat. What next? You hire some children to reenact my life in full? You are pathetic."

Vadim stops short, his teeth clattering together, his eyes like ebony fire.

"Copy you?" he wonders coldly. "By womanizing and terrorizing? Don't kid yourself. Hire children? I've known my limits in ways you can't even imagine. I was not so reckless as to gamble a young life to placate my 'whores' or assuage my ego—"

He cocks his head and smiles that beautiful, breathtaking grin. It's wider than ever, quivering at the edges. Meanwhile, his eyes blaze, a chilling ebony. "How long before your happy little family falls apart by your own making?"

"Son of a bitch!" Maxim's arms ripple with tension as he starts to circle around the table. "Is that a threat?"

"Maxim," Francesca says, rising from her chair. Her eyes worriedly trace his shuddering frame, but if I'm not mistaken, he stops short, his breaths thundering from his chest like growls.

"Get out," he snarls.

"Why should I?" Vadim counters. "I do own part of it, after all."

"An oversight." Maxim shoots a glare in Milton's direction, implying something I suspect. Vadim mentioned that he owned part of the sex club—but I'm realizing that partnership may not be mutual on Maxim's end. "One I will soon rectify if I have to beat a 'recusal' out of you. You think I'll let you weasel your way into my life? My club? You should have stayed in the shadows, rat. Sniveling in secret suits you better than playing the part of a man!"

He lunges, but Vadim doesn't move. He doesn't even blink. I've never seen him like this. Enraged. Frozen. Paralyzed. Social etiquette would dictate I try to smooth things over—but something in my brain snaps, and all of my social conditioning goes right out of the darn window.

"S-Stop!" I step forward in the path of the advancing man, though Milton is already behind him, placing a restraining hand on his shoulder.

"Have you forgotten what we discussed?" Milton says quickly, his grip tight as he glares at the back of his skull. But Maxim's clearly too angry to see anything other than Vadim in his firing line.

"Leave him alone," I rasp anyway. "We're going—"

"Ah, so you've trained her to defend you," Maxim sneers, his mouth a fearsome snarl. "One would think you'd repulse any woman with an ounce of sense. It must be the money. Pathetic. I hope you reward her well for this stunt."

My vision blurs as anger sears through my skin. I think something in my brain snaps, robbing me of any semblance of decorum. I don't even realize I'm speaking until my voice echoes back to me, high-pitched and bitchy.

"What the hell is wrong with you?" A better question would be—why am I so angry? Why does the sight of Vadim standing rigid make something inside of me tear open and bleed? I can't explain it. I can't suppress it. Facing down Maxim, I grit my teeth and square my shoulders, unafraid. "All he wants is a relationship with you! Can't you see that?"

I can. I can acknowledge the effort it took for him to even come here. His barely concealed confusion that I had scored a customary present from his brother, who only seemed to treat him with hate. I don't know what lurks between them. Heck, I don't even know the man beside me. But with my hand in his grip, I can't seem to back down, even as he tugs me toward him, his voice a slap, "Come. We're leaving—"

"Why are you such an ass to him?" I demand, though I've heard the horrific actions mentioned. Kidnapping. Threats. But Vadim's scar looms vibrant in my mind. His pain when he speaks of his past. The longing he doesn't even seem to realize whenever he brings up his brother. Is it all rooted in hateful malice? No. I don't think so.

"Do you have any idea how much he just wants to be accepted by you?"

Maxim blinks, his nostrils flaring, eyes widening.

And I have my answer.

"You don't do you? You don't have a clue—"

"*Tiffany!*"

I flinch in response to Vadim's tone. It's icier than I've ever heard it—a stranger's, adrift on an island to himself. "We're leaving. Now."

He releases my hand and storms toward the entrance, leaving me to follow.

"Dima," Milton calls after him. It seems he's about to go after him, but the blond takes his hand and stops him, her eyes pleading with something I can't even begin to understand. Only now do I realize that everyone is staring at me. Open-mouthed. All I can do is spin on my heels and chase the lanky figure marching steadily toward the red sportscar out front.

He holds out the door for me, but as I pass him and enter the passenger's side, I suck in a breath, chilled to the bone. He's *angry*. Furious.

My heart pounds as he claims the driver's seat, his expression a mystery in the dark.

"Did you really do it?" I croak as he slams on the gas, sending us careening down the driveway. "Did you kidnap a little girl?"

I don't sound anywhere near as horrified as I should. Maybe because I already know the answer before he clenches his jaw, his gaze fathomless.

"Yes."

He did. A man who seems to enjoy needling his brother through any means had no qualms with using a child as a pawn in their game. But is it really so simple?

"Why?" I ask, struggling to understand.

He shrugs, and his haughty chuckle should give me my answer. "Take your pick of one of the many horrific explanations circling your brain," he suggests coldly. "You know my past. I'm sure you're jumping to that conclusion—"

"Don't you dare." I square my jaw and shift to face him though he doesn't look from the road once. "Don't insult me. Don't shut me out. You did it. I'm willing to hear why. So tell me." Something in how he stiffens makes me add, "I know you wouldn't hurt her... You wouldn't."

Maybe it's naive, but when I picture him with Zzazza—his affinity for such an innocent creature—I can't see him hurting a child, not even to spite Maxim. Even as I watch, he flinches at the insinuation, betraying his own disgust at the accusation.

"You didn't," I insist, surer of that by the second. "I want the truth."

"I..." He deflates, his posture wavering. "I wanted to know," he finally confesses, his voice soft. "I wanted to know."

"What?" I whisper. Gathering up enough nerve, I tentatively stroke his forearm. He's as rigid as stone, stiffening against me. "Tell me."

He laughs, and his wall comes up in record speed. Stunned, I recoil, withdrawing from him.

"Don't pretend like you aren't suspecting what I know you are—"

"Stop it!" I lower my hand, this time resisting the impulse to recoil. "Stop pushing me away."

"Why?" he counters, more harshly than ever.

"Because I know you," I say simply, though deep down, I know how false that statement may be. But in some ways, it's not. I feel it in a way I've never been so sure about anything before. Jim was an asshole. Vadim is far from it—though he likes to play the part of one. "I don't think you would hurt a child. Not with the way you treat Zzazza—and if you did, I think Maxim would have killed you," I add with a hard swallow. "You had to have a reason, and I'd like to think it's deeper than trying to spite your dick of a brother."

He goes silent, still stewing. Still brooding. Still so very angry.

But as his eyes flicker from the road for an instant, I sense for the first time that I'm not who he's angry at. Not by a longshot.

"I wanted to know," he reiterates, his voice a hollow rasp. "If I... How... If I could be around her. If she could sense that I was broken. If I had made the right choice. And I did then. I know I did. I *know*." His voice breaks, conveying such pain...

Tears prick my eyes before I can fight them back, drawn by the fierceness of his reaction.

"The choice to what?"

"To leave her," he says, devoid of any emotion. "To abandon her. I let her go. I had to... I had to."

I don't think he's talking about Maxim's little girl anymore—or anyone I'm familiar with. Another woman? I don't have the heart to ask about her now. He's more distant from me than ever.

"Vadim?" I brush my hand along his forearm.

He wrenches away from me violently, and the car jolts sideways with the force of his reaction. I brace my hand against the dashboard as he navigates through the city, and after what feels like an eternity, we finally reach his home.

He parks and leaves the car before I can get my bearings. I'm forced to trail him into the house, unsure of whether to even stay.

Vadim is gone. His body may be here, but his soul is eons away. I risk whispering his name, but he doesn't even look at me. He crosses to the bar and hunches over it, his face in his hands, his body trembling.

"You should eat something," I suggest, taking a tentative step forward.

"I need to be alone."

His tone is a slap. Confused, I turn to the stairs and hurry up them without letting myself reconcile the fact that I should leave. Staying at all is foolish. We aren't in a relationship. He owes me nothing.

And I'm not responsible for soothing his boo-boos or fighting his battles. I tell myself this even as I enter the closet and exchange my dress for an ivory nightgown. When I approach the bed, Vadim isn't there waiting for me.

He doesn't come up the stairs when I lie down, either.

And I remain awake, listening for him until I finally hear his steps resonate…

But they depart the house entirely.

And a door slams in his wake.

CHAPTER TWENTY-TWO

He doesn't return by the time dawn creeps across the horizon, and I drag myself from the bed and venture downstairs. It's eerily silent, and the excessive neatness of the house stands out in stark contrast to the chaos of storm clouds building beyond the windows. On second appraisal, the place looks barely lived in.

There are no pictures. No personal knickknacks. Despite my sex toy, I don't think I can name anything in the house that stands out as remotely unique.

The man is living in a dollhouse.

And yet I sense that he picked it—specifically this location—for a reason. To further torment his brother? Out of some unhealthy interest in the children Maxim lives with? Or is it more than that?

Something to deal with *her*. The person he mentioned abandoning. Someone from his past?

Jealousy, that vicious thing, nibbles away at my resolve. From his tone alone, I sense *she* mattered to him more than I could ever dream to. I've never heard his voice so…broken before. So vulnerable and raw.

So imperfectly human.

I'm tempted to venture up to the room he warned me against. Maybe the answer lurks in there? I shrug off the thought, though.

My past is an animal I feel comfortable dredging up only on my terms. I sense he might feel the same way.

So, I'll wait, and stew in self-pity instead. Ena was right. I'm an idiot toy, and I couldn't even do something as simple as make sure the darn man ate. I picture him wandering mindlessly, his blood sugar dangerously low—or high. And it's all my fault.

Cooking was never my forte, but I enter the kitchen and find myself fishing ingredients from his surprisingly well-stocked kitchen. This must be Ena's realm. I try to tread carefully as I dump a handful of ingredients into a bowl, too distracted to measure properly. I merely work on autopilot until I pour some semblance of a batter into a cake pan just as the front door opens, carrying a familiar scent.

I shove my cake attempt into the oven and race from behind the counter. Vadim is already entering the kitchen, still wearing his suit from last night, his face haggard. His eyes take me in, and gradually his wall lowers.

I pull out a stool and silently urge him onto it. Sighing, he complies, shifting to face me as I circle the counter.

I'm painfully aware of his eyes on the back of my neck, tracking my progress as I wash each dish and return them to their rightful spot. By the time I'm done, a promising smell issues from the oven.

I check on my cake and warily pull it out. When I turn holding my offering, Vadim raises an eyebrow.

"Breakfast," I say awkwardly as I set the cake before him. "It won't taste as good as Ena's, but you need to eat something." I hunt for a fork, stab it into the center of my cake and warily offer it to him.

He meets my gaze for so long my legs have gone numb by the time he finally accepts the fork and takes a bite.

"It's good," he lies, struggling to choke down my creation. To my shock, he drags the cake closer to him and goes in for another bite.

A relieved sigh nearly robs me of balance. I have to brace my hands against the counter just to stay upright. "I'm sorry," I blurt. "I shouldn't have run my mouth. I shouldn't have said—"

"Don't." He sounds so tired. "Don't ever apologize to me. You've earned that right. No one—but perhaps Milton—has ever defended me like that against him," he adds thickly. "No one."

He makes it sound so momentous—arguing with an, albeit very scary, dickhead who seems determined to rip him down for whatever reason. He's having another one of those revelations, I suspect—but this one is dangerous, because I think I'm sharing the same moment of awe.

Such a beautiful, broken man who doesn't realize he's worth defending. Protecting.

"Don't shut me out like that again," I whisper. I'm begging. "Don't. You scared me."

"I know." He looks away and rakes a trembling hand through his hair, his expression pained. "I know…"

"Next time, I just won't force-feed you a horrible cake that may or may not give you unintended food poisoning, either."

His lip quirks, forming a shadow of that trademark grin. "Next time?"

"Yes," I say, deciding something momentous on a moment's whim. There's no turning back now. "I want a relationship with you. A real one, if you're interested, that is…"

He looks away, and my heart seizes up. Panic, unlike any other, grips me tight, and I realize just how badly I do want to explore something with him. Something beyond sex. Something real?

"Do I want it?" he echoes softly. His slim fingers flatten over the counter as he stands. "Turn around."

I frown but comply, sensing an urgency that warns me not to question. His breath fans the back of my neck as he approaches me from behind and smooths the hair from my neck. Something flashes before my eyes, and I sense a coolness settle against my throat. I reach up instinctively and gasp as my fingers fall over a delicate, silver chain.

"Vadim," I whisper, my voice shaking. "It's beautiful."

A diamond necklace beyond my gold-digging dreams. It's decadent and yet delicate, and I know without even having to ask that it must have cost him a fortune.

"You didn't have to buy me anything," I start, but his hand settles over my shoulder, making me fall silent.

"I know…" At the sound of his voice, I spin around to find his gaze stormier than ever. He strokes my cheek, cradling my jaw against his palm. "Think of it as a down payment in my quest to earn your affections," he adds. I notice that nearby a baby blue box rests on the counter. The same one he'd taunted me with the other night.

A tiny prickle of unease stabs in my chest—the same feeling I got when he thought I was an escort. Beautiful or not, the gift is yet another subtle insinuation that our interactions are only ever a transaction to him. He once claimed that communication was merely another form of manipulation. Does he think I'm only interested in him in exchange for bribes and toys? Even his brother had insinuated as much.

"You don't like it?" He frowns and copies me by eyeing the box. "I can return it—"

"No!" Shaking my head to banish the doubts, I lean forward, letting my lips settle over his. "Don't return it. But I do have rules," I confess as his lips part against mine, and his hand slides around to the back of my skull, dragging me close.

"Oh?" He chuckles, his eyebrow raised. "Do state your proposal clearly."

I reach down to finger his tie. "I want you to be open with me," I murmur, loosening the silken strip. "I want you to trust me. I want you to be kinky with me whenever I command."

"Ah, very tough conditions." He draws back and grasps my hips. I arch into him. Gosh, I hadn't realized just how much I'd craved his touch. A night without him and already the withdrawal was unbearable.

"I want to comfort you when you're hurting," I whisper, my eyes closing. "Don't shut me out. You are not repulsive to me. I... I want you—"

He silences me with a kiss so deep my head spins as I relax into his arms, letting my hands roam his body as my hips seek out the firmness straining the front of his slacks. He feels so good against me. I can't get over it.

Drunk on his scent, I match his vigor and palm him through the fabric of his pants, drawing a beautiful groan from his throat. And yet, he captures my wrist, preventing me from freeing him.

"Ena will kill me if we soil his kitchen," he grates, guiding me back toward the doorway. "I think it's about time I came up to bed, anyway."

"No." At the base of the stairs, I slide my fingers beneath his jacket. "I need you now."

He stiffens as I tug at his pants, only to watch me with dawning understanding as I drag them down his hips and free his cock from the confines of his briefs. He's hard already, stiffening against my touch. His hands cinch my waist as he pivots, pressing me against the wall while I eagerly wrap my leg around him.

He enters me slowly, and I savor the way my body adjusts. Like I was made for him. Designed to conform around him—so expertly, he fits me like a key sliding into a specially crafted lock. My eyes flutter shut, but he strokes my chin, forcing me to meet his heavy-lidded gaze.

"Stay with me," he murmurs while thrusting so darn deep. "I need you to look at me, beautiful. Stay with me."

He's pleading as his eyes scan mine for something—though I'm not sure what. Something that makes my head rear back, my eyes threatening to roll. Only for them to fly open in shock as he withdraws, leaving me aching and gaping.

It's only after my gaze returns to his that he starts to move. Again. Harder. More.

"So good," I tell him, sensing now more than ever that he needs to hear this. Know this. "You feel so good, baby. So good. So good."

He grunts, snatching my hips toward him, altering his angle of attack.

I cry out, gasping iterations of his name as my nails sink into his hair. I know even as my body clamps down around him, trembling with release, that I'm far beyond the danger zone when it comes to him. I think I've been past the point of return for days now.

I burry my mouth into the crook of his shoulder, stroking his back as he slams into me, inching my body up the wall with every thrust. I never knew sex could be like this.

Raw.

Real.

Intoxicating.

We're experiencing something more than just a sharing of bodies. Something primal that makes me cling to him long after my orgasm rips me apart.

So much for finding a billionaire to screw for the weekend. Vadim Gorgoshev has shattered those simple expectations. This moment cements that whatever we share is already far beyond that.

And far more than my sexual adventure is at stake.

I'm falling for him.

Hard.

And from this height, I don't see any soft landing in sight.

HE BATHES ME AGAIN, massaging my limbs while I lie prone on the shower bench at his mercy. The water has long since stopped running—triggered by an automatic shutoff from what I could tell. A warm haze of steam bathes everything in a soft, dreamy blur, misting our skin and fogging our glass surroundings.

We're in our own private universe, one I never want to leave.

"Your body is a masterpiece," Vadim says, his voice a low rasp. I shiver as he drags a rag across my lower back as if memorizing every divot and curve.

"Why, Mr. Gorgoshev!" I exclaim with mock alarm. "Is that a compliment? Dare I say praise?"

He smiles, and it's breathtaking. I make a mental note to never allow him near his asshole of a brother again. No one is worth making him lose this smile.

"Or should I call you Dima?" I wonder, recalling the moniker Milton and his brother used.

I instantly regret the suggestion as his face falls flat.

"No," he says, stroking up the curve of my spine. "I… I love the way you say my name."

My grin is a mile wide, and I attempt to practice my sexy purr, "You mean like this? *Vadim.*"

He nods, his nostrils flaring. "Like that."

I roll onto my back and observe him leisurely, drinking in every inch of his gorgeous frame.

"Will you pierce me now?" I wonder as he turns his attention to my torso. He skirts the cloth between my breasts, traveling down over my belly.

"Now?" He releases an appreciative sigh as his gaze lowers to my legs. "Perhaps," he says. "You still want this?"

I grin wickedly. "More than ever."

Something equally feral alights his gaze as he stands and pulls me into his arms. Cool air assaults us both when he finally opens the shower stall, and we forsake the warmth for a brisk return to the real world. On his way into the bedroom, he grabs a handful of towels and dries me off before letting me crawl onto the mattress.

I twist around, reaching for him. "Are you going to do naughty, sexy things to me before I'm pierced?" I wonder, my voice giddy.

"I—" A crisp, musical tone cuts him off. Confused, we both turn to the nightstand where his cell phone rests. It dawns on me that I've never heard it ring before. The novelty of the fact makes him frown, and I suspect it's not by accident. Few people must have that number, their calls unavoidable. "I have to take this," he says reluctantly, crossing over to the end table.

I lie back and watch as he casually answers, only for his posture to shift drastically in the space of a heartbeat. He hunches over, gripping the end of the table, his voice hoarse. "T-Tomorrow? No, I understand. Yes, I am still interested. Placement?"

He exhales raggedly, tearing his hand through his hair, and I rise up to my knees, concerned.

"What's wrong?" I ask when he finally hangs up.

He averts his gaze, his expression drawn tight. His stupid wall comes up, up, up, and I feel like a madwoman desperately trying to tear it back down.

"No! Don't!" I shuffle toward him and loop my arms around his neck, pressing my body to his. "Don't shut me out. You don't have to tell me everything, but just give me a hint. Don't shut me out."

"A hint?" He sounds so damn exhausted. I lean back, pulling him onto the bed, forcing him to lie beside me. He stares up at the ceiling while I straddle him, stroking his cheek. Finally, his eyes refocus on me, and hesitation transforms his features. He almost looks like a stranger again. Some new man with new secrets to uncover. "I will need my fake wife tomorrow," he confesses.

Jealousy rises up so swiftly I can't suppress it—until I remember. I don't recall him actually hiring anyone to fulfill that role. In fact...the ring is still on my finger, so comfortable there I'd forgotten I've been wearing it all this time. Leaning down, I claim his mouth and drag my fingers down his front.

"Me," I tell him sternly. "I'll be your fake wife." I simper, pleased with myself, but his frown deepens, his gaze still distant.

"There is something I need to tell you," he says seriously. "But I don't think you'll stay if I do."

I shudder at the thought of what. A real wife that he needs a decoy in order to divorce from? Legal trouble, and he needs a wife as a character witness? My brain churns through the possibilities, but I can't think of any dire enough to make him look so...

Torn.

I come to a decision too quickly to parse through the consequences. "Then don't tell me," I say, sealing the request with a kiss. "Not yet. I think I can handle anything—but murder, a secret army of bastard children, or my participation in a ponzi scheme—" I break off as he jolts upright, knocking me off of him.

Dazed, I roll onto my side and watch him. He's cradling his face in both hands, his expression stricken.

"I said something wrong," I whisper, reaching for him. "I'm sorry. What did I say—"

"Nothing." He stands and marches into the bathroom, his shoulders hunched against me. "I... I'll be back."

I slump against the pillows, blinking as my eyes burn. I'm stung by the whiplash of his reaction, but more than that, I'm worried. For him. He's flickering like a candle flame now more than ever. I don't know which direction to swing in to match him. Playful? Serious? Sensual?

I still haven't decided by the time he reappears in the doorway, his hair dripping, his face damp. I imagine him standing over the sink, splashing water onto his face until he regained his trademark composure. His dark eyes flicker to me, wholly unreadable.

"Stay," he commands before entering the hallway, his footsteps resonating. Puzzled, I wait once again in anticipation of which way the flame of his mood will dance. Seconds later, his voice drifts back to me, "Come."

I stand and follow after him on unsteady legs. He's just down the hall, in the closed room directly adjacent to the bedroom. The space beyond is just as massive though sparsely furnished.

Cardboard boxes are stacked in one corner, each one large and sufficiently mysterious. In the center of the room is a leather chaise with a sheet draped over it. Nearby is a metal folding table upon which is an array of neat, surgical-looking supplies set on top of another white cloth.

Standing with enviable grace, Vadim tugs on a pair of gloves with his back to me.

"Are you ready to accept this?" he wonders, his tone sin.

I quiver, my heart racing with excitement. "Ready to accept what?" I ask innocently as I continue to close the distance between us.

So maybe he wasn't lying about being a trained professional. His setup looks sterile and organized with clinical precision.

"Impressive," I murmur, stroking his shoulder. He cocks his head back, a quick, tempered smile playing over his lips.

Whatever upset him before is apparently forgotten.

"Sit," he commands, gesturing to the chaise. "I need to examine you."

A thrill runs through me as I practically hop onto the surface and lie back while lifting my nightgown up to my hips. He turns to survey me, his gaze narrowed with focus. Shyly, I spread my legs, giggling as he sucks in a breath. Yet overall, he maintains his steely, doctorly presence.

"Have you ever been pierced before, Ms. Connors?" he wonders while unfolding a medical drape that he places over my abdomen.

"Just my ears," I reply.

A low sound resonates in his chest as he urges my legs apart and instructs me to bend my knees. "*Merde*," he grates, an unprofessional term. Not that I care. The expression on his face… It's enough to make me bite my lip and consider putting this off long enough to seduce him. His eyes are wide, his lips parted and deliciously pink. I inhale as they move, his voice a low hum, "You are so beautiful."

I'm drunk off his baritone, dizzy already. Having him peer between my legs is surprisingly more comfortable than I feel it should be. More intimate. He eyes me appreciatively but in a way that doesn't make me feel like a piece of meat. What was that word he used?

Masterpiece.

I shudder as he guides me further into the correct position. Then he changes his gloves to a fresh pair and swipes a cool liquid over my mound, fighting to regain his professional composure.

"You will feel some pain," he warns as he turns back to his selection of tools. He lifts something delicately with a pair of tweezers and holds it up for my inspection. "Is this fitting enough to meet your expectations?"

"Oh, Vadim," I breathe as I take in the delicately curved piece of metal—the female equivalent to his barbell piercing. "It's beautiful."

I watch eagerly as he manipulates his tools and captures the tiny hood of flesh above my clitoris. But as I hold my breath in anticipation, his doctorly persona slips.

"Tell me you want this," he commands in a gruffer baritone, meeting my gaze. *This.* That dangerous word contains so many unspoken entities, each one hinted at by the ferocity making his eyes seem to glow.

And I don't hesitate. "I want this."

Wordlessly, he guides a needle through a corresponding tool and then sets the piercing in place. The needle drives in easily, but despite any numbing he may have used, the pressure is uncomfortable as hell. I grit my teeth, hissing at the sensation. Thankfully, the discomfort quickly fades into awed admiration as I watch the piercing mark my flesh. A statement of independence if there ever was one. A slight bit of pressure exists but isn't unbearable, and as Vadim guides me to my feet, I don't feel too much discomfort.

"No tight clothing for the first week, at least," he warns, as any professional would. "To err on the side of caution, no rigorous sex for the same timeframe either. Four to eight weeks at most is the typical healing timeframe."

I pout. "But what shall I tell all of the many horny billionaires wrapped around my finger?"

He frowns as if seriously mulling it over. "Tell them that you are taken," he suggests, pulling me into his arms. "That you are *owned*."

"Owned?" I play with the word on my tongue. It surprisingly doesn't sound anywhere near as degrading as it should. More than that. Powerful. Owned the way the moon owns the strength of the ocean's tides—both drawn to each other in an inescapable, magnetic pull. "There is one billionaire in particular who demands satisfaction," I tell him, standing on tiptoe so I can whisper into his ear. "I don't think he'll want to wait a whole week to enjoy me."

"Oh?" his tone lowers to that dangerous, devious baritone.

I nod, sliding my tongue along my lower lip. "Oh, yes. I suppose I'll just have to find other ways to pleasure him in the meantime. Starting with…" I blurt out an array of x-rated suggestions, and he laughs, throwing his head back, his eyes gleaming.

"It's a good thing I took the liberty of special-ordering a few apparatuses specifically for that occasion." He gestures to the boxes in the corner, and my eyes go wide.

"A kinky room, just for me? Why Vadim, I didn't know if you had the imagination in you."

"And then some," he warns, his upper lip quirked. "You'd be surprised what a quick Google search and an hour's long consultation with one of the world's most renowned sexual experts can accomplish…"

CHAPTER TWENTY-THREE

It isn't until midnight that he turns distant again. I catch him brooding through half-closed eyes, and I doubt he's even aware that I'm watching him. His brows are drawn together, his expression stricken. Two slim fingers massage his temples to no avail. With every passing second, his frown deepens, enhancing the uniqueness of his face that lends to sadness so well. To torment.

I start to reach for him, but he turns away, lying with his back to me. And I know that whatever is bothering him has everything to do with our newfound relationship. Regret?

But why?

I'm too terrified to seek out an answer now. Not freshly pierced and drunk off lust. I drift off instead, and it's morning when I finally startle awake.

"I need you dressed."

I look over to find Vadim exiting the closet, already wearing a suit. Over his arm is an array of brightly colored fabric that must be an outfit for me.

"Please," he urges, spreading out a tweed coral skirt and ruby blouse onto the end of the mattress.

"What's going on?" I blink my eyes to adjust to the harsh daylight as I sit upright. My piercing aches, but not in an overly painful way. More like a giddy reminder of the hedonistic pledge I made to both him and myself—owned. My brain melts at the memory, and I almost miss what he says next.

"My…meeting." He cuts his gaze to the door and tugs at his tie. "They are almost here."

He's nervous, I realize. It's such a contrast to his usual icy cool that it takes me longer to process it.

"Okay." I bound into the bathroom and wash up quickly. Then I change into the clothing he specified, puzzled by the overall effect—modest, yet fashionable. The perfect perky wife to his cold businessman. When I stand beside him, I envision the picture we make.

And I freaking love it.

A posh businessman and his classy, yet sexy wife. My heart aches as I realize just how much I enjoy the thought of it. Being his, displayed on his arm. Belonging to someone who seems eager to show me off rather than make me wilt in his shadow.

I smooth my hand down his shoulder, startled when he pulls away.

"I need to tell you—" He breaks off, his body angled away from me so that I can't see his face. Puzzled, I reach for him again.

"What's wrong?"

He cocks his head and moves swiftly toward the hall. "They're here."

They? I follow him warily, lingering in his wake. Downstairs, a stern-faced Ena stands guard near the foyer. The two men share a glance, conveying a silent understanding. As Vadim nods in approval, Ena opens the door, revealing the woman I recognize from his lunch "meeting" the other day. Today her outfit is an olive green two-piece suit ensemble with a modest-fitting jacket and skirt.

"Good morning," she says with a tight smile, stepping inside. "I'm so glad you could accommodate us at such short notice. *We* are glad. Aren't we, Magdalene?"

Vadim descends the final few steps and crosses to her, his voice deeper and more tense than ever. "Of course…" He trails off as a smaller figure appears beside the woman.

And I nearly fall down the rest of the stairs.

The girl—so small she can be only six or seven at most—looks like a living doll she's so beautiful. Curling black hair frames a face set with delicate features. *Familiar* features.

That nose. That chin. That surly, brooding frown. I can't even believe it at first—but as I blink, I realize my eyes aren't lying. The only difference between her and the man standing a few paces away are her eyes, a bright, vibrant blue.

But there is no mistaking the obvious. Genetics are a strange animal—two people couldn't just strike the same biological jackpot by chance.

This little girl is his. She has to be…

His *daughter.*

And I realize—just like I did the night he used me to taunt his brother—that once again, I've been a pawn in his game. A fool. Because any relationship he claimed to want with me was based on nothing more than a twisted lie.

<u>Vadim's story continues in Corrupt!</u>

A WORD FROM THE AUTHOR

Hey there!

Thank you so much for reading! If you enjoyed the story, please leave a review and recommend the book to any friend you think would love this twisted world. You'd have my eternal gratitude. Even a short sentence goes a long way!

Then, come join the rest of us dark romance lovers in my Facebook Group where you can get snippets, sneak peeks of upcoming books and even help vote on aspects of future novels.

Come to the dark side:
https://www.facebook.com/groups/lanasbeautifulmonsters/

WANT MORE STUFF TO READ?
Join my newsletter and get a **free book**! Plus, you get to stay updated with any new releases, random giveaways and exclusive sneak peeks!
https://www.lanaskybooks.com/newsletter

Other Novels: https://lanaskybooks.com/

Lana Sky is a reclusive writer in the United States who spends most of her time daydreaming about complex male characters and parenting her Cockapoo Joey. She writes dark, twisted romance across several genres. Her titles include everything from mafia romance to vampires.